FOUND.

FOUND.

a novel

t. rigney

iUniverse, Inc.
New York Lincoln Shanghai

found.

a novel

iUniverse, Inc.

For information address:
iUniverse, Inc.
2021 Pine Lake Road, Suite 100
Lincoln, NE 68512
www.iuniverse.com

ISBN: 0-595-33064-9

Printed in the United States of America

for theresa.

my wife.

my muse.

this never could have happened without you.

CONTENTS

▼

Chapter 1

▼

Secrets

My brother keeps a human head in his closet.

He keeps it in his bowling ball bag. I don't know what he did with the bowling ball, though. I haven't seen it around his room lately. He must have thrown it away. That's how I found it, you know. I was going bowling with my friends and I wanted to borrow his ball but he wasn't home. So I took it without asking him permission, which is a no-no. When I opened the bag at the alley I almost cried. I didn't tell anyone about it and used my friend's ball instead. I lied and said the one I brought was too heavy for me. I'm surprised they couldn't smell it.

When he's at work I take it out and look at it. I use my mother's yellow rubber gloves because I don't want to get blood on my hands. Every few days he has a new head. Usually they're black women. One time he had a white man's head in there. The eyes were missing and his tongue was sticking out.

I threw up in the toilet after that one.

Today there's another black woman in here. Her eyes are open like someone surprised her. I've seen lots of horror movies and the heads in those things don't come close to looking like the real thing. I can't explain what it feels like to hold one of them. At one point it had thoughts and feelings and it kissed someone it loved. Now it's just a bloody head in a bowling ball bag. I hope I don't end up that way.

If my brother ever found out I came in here he'd probably kill me, too. That's what scares me. What if he does find out? What if he comes home and looks at the head and I put it back in the bag facing the wrong direction? If he's a killer he probably thinks about things like that because he's crazy. The first person he'd blame would be me. Big brothers blame little brothers for everything. Dad says that's just the way it is.

I get home before everyone else because I go to school and they go to work. Dad works on computers, Mom works at an office doing stuff I don't understand, and my big brother works at a factory where they make soda pop. Sometimes he brings us free drinks. I don't know if he steals them or not.

Whenever I'm home alone I go through my family's private things. Mom keeps all her old love letters from Dad under her bed. Dad keeps his dirty magazines in a big shoe box in the back of his closet. And I've already said what my brother keeps hidden in his closet. Mom and Dad would flip if they ever found out he was keeping human heads in the house. That would get him kicked out for sure.

I hear a car pull up outside. Rocks and dirt from the driveway crunch really loud under my Mom's mini-van. I use that sound as a signal to put my brother's secret things back in his secret hiding place. I rush to the bathroom and wash the blood off the gloves and put them back under the sink. By the time she's inside and calling my name, I'm in the living room watching cartoons like a good boy. She doesn't have any idea what's going on inside her own house. I think it's better that way.

"Marty!" she says in a stern voice. I'm in trouble already. "I've been calling your name since I came through the door. Can you help me with the groceries?"

"You went to the grocery?" I ask. That's usually a weekend chore.

"Yeah." She sounds tired and irritated. "I took off early and got it out of the way. Come on. Get off the couch and help me."

I help her carry the plastic bags into the house. She got me Cheese Nips. They're my favorite thing in the whole wide world. I could eat these things until my stomach pops open and the gooey orange gunk comes oozing out the hole. And while everyone was screaming and pointing at the gross stuff coming out of me, I'd just keep right on eating those Cheese Nips. I've never tasted anything so good.

Mom tells me about her day while we put the food away. Her boss called her stupid today because she messed up some kind of report. When she tried to explain what happened he called her a "stupid woman who needed to get her stuff together." Although he didn't really say stuff. He said shit. Mom doesn't like to use dirty words so she uses good words to substitute for the bad ones. She says fudge when she means fuck. I don't know why she does it. Dad cusses everyday.

When she asks me about my day, I tell her about my test. Math is hard, but math tests are harder because you have to use what you've learned in order to pass. I'm not very good at remembering stuff so I have to use study notes the night before. One time I cheated on a test, but I ended up telling the teacher what I did. She told me she was proud of me for admitting it. Then she called my mom and I got grounded.

After I'm done telling her about the test I tell her about the comic book I drew. I like to draw cartoons, usually really weird superheroes that I've come up with on my own. I've got one guy who dresses up like a giant roach. His name is Roach-Man. And I've got a guy who wears a brown paper sack over his head because he's so ugly. I call him Bag Lunch. They're always fighting each other in this really big city somewhere in the United States. I haven't come up with a name for it yet.

Dad says he doesn't like my comics because they're too violent. I draw them in black-and-white but I use a red color pencil for the blood. And there's always lots of blood. Now that I know what a severed head looks like I draw them all the time in my books. People are always getting decapitated.

The telephone rings. Mom answers it.

I read the back of the Cheese Nips box while I sit at the table. I try not to listen to her conversation because that's called eavesdropping. I really can't help it, though. It takes about two minutes for her to say the person's name. Grandma. Of course it's Grandma. She's always calling about something. Doesn't matter if it's one in the morning or five in the evening, if Grandma has something to say she's going to call you and say it. I hate the sound of our telephone at night. It echoes really loud in my room.

Mom says goodbye and hangs up the phone. She looks at me, smiles, and sits down at the table. Then she leans in close.

"Do you wanna hear something really gross?" she asks.

"Yeah!" I love her gross stories. Dad doesn't like it when she tells me these stories, so she does it when he's at work. We have an agreement.

"Grandma just saw on television where a guy in Lexington ripped out his eyes when the cops were trying to arrest him." She pretends like she might be sick. This makes me laugh. "Isn't that gross?"

"Yeah," I say, giggling. "That's pretty gross."

"I thought you could use that for your comics," she says with a wink. I give her a wink back. That's one of our little things we do. What's really weird is that she has a problem with me watching horror movies. And even though my dad doesn't like the violence in my comics or Mom's bloody stories, he doesn't mind letting me watch horror movies. My parents are really, really weird. Sometimes I don't think they really know what they're doing. Just look at my brother.

"David said they're called graphic novels," I tell her. David is one of the people I show my books to at school. He's also one of the only kids who will talk to me. "I told him I just thought they were called comic books."

"What are graphic novels?" my mom asks. She's getting things ready for dinner. "Does that mean they're really graphic?"

"I think it means they use pictures," I say with a shrug. "I dunno."

We talk about television, movies, and school.

Until my brother walks through the door.

Steve and my parents have a strange relationship. My mom gives him weird smiles like she's really trying her hardest to force that smile out. Dad just ignores him most of the time, unless it's to yell at him for parking his car in the driveway. It leaks oil so he makes Steve park it along the curb out front. Sometimes Steve forgets to park it there and Dad starts yelling. Then they usually start fighting.

It happens at least once a week.

I think it's because they're disappointed in Steve. He flunked out of college in the first year because he spent too much time drinking beer and "chasing skirt." That's what my Dad calls dating, my mom says. I think it means something else, though. My parents were really upset about him flunking since it cost so much to put him through school. That would make me angry, too.

Steve walks right through the kitchen and into the hallway. He doesn't speak to either of us. Not a single word.

"Hi to you, too," Mom says to herself, but it's loud enough for me to hear.

Steve stops in the hallway.

"I said hi," he says. Then he goes upstairs to his room.

Mom starts to cry.

"What are we having for dinner?" I ask.

"Chicken," she says. She keeps crying.

"And?" I ask. We usually have chicken and mashed potatoes. Or chicken and biscuits. Or chicken and some sort of vegetable. But when she said chicken it made me worry. Chicken doesn't fill me up by itself. I need something to go with it.

"Is that all?" I ask.

"Go watch television, Marty," she says. My name is Martin but everyone calls me Marty, like in *Back To The Future* with Michael J. Fox. We have that on DVD. My brother got it for me for Christmas last year.

Mom doesn't like to talk about things when she's upset. I don't, either. But if I'm upset about something she's always asking me what's wrong. She knows I don't like to talk about things. I like to figure stuff out on my own. It makes me feel more grown-up. Mom and I are a lot alike. Dad says that all the time. I wonder if that makes him sad. He and Steve are a lot alike, though. Except for the severed heads. They both have really bad tempers and they're not very patient.

I go into the living room and turn on the TV. Nothing's on. I flip through the channels, but there's still nothing I want to watch. In the kitchen I can hear her crying. Sometimes I want to tell her about the heads in the closet, but I think that will only make things worse. And the last thing I want to do is make things worse between Mom and Dad and Steve. Why can't we be happy likes in *The Cosby Show*? Where all of our problems are always solved when the show is over.

Unless it's a two-part episode.

I nap until Dad gets home.

Then we all sit down to dinner.

CHAPTER 2

▼

FAMILY

Dad always sits at the head of the table.

On the right-hand side of the table is Mom. They look so different. Dad is tall and fit and handsome while Mom is short and blonde and just kinda plain. I like going out with Mom to the mall. We blend into the crowds and I like that. Whenever Dad comes with us women have a tendency to stare. Mom hates it, but that's what you get when you marry a handsome man. At least that's what I think.

I sit on the left-hand side. I'm kinda plain, too, but I've got a big nose that comes to a point. The kids at school all look at me like I'm a freak, and Larry Johnson calls me Banana Nose. Sometimes I just stare at it in the mirror and wonder if anyone notices anything else about me when they look at my face.

I bet they don't.

Steve's a lot better looking than I am. I can't remember a time when he didn't have a girlfriend of some sort. Now he just kills them. I always thought it was the ugly people that killed people and put their heads in bowling ball bags. Not the good-looking, square-jawed, shaggy-haired factory workers who still live at home. The people who write horror movies really don't know anything.

Our dining room is a part of our living room. We can sit at the dinner table and watch television if we wanted to, but Dad thinks it's a good time for everyone to sit down and talk about things. Like about what we did that day or whatever. Usually my parents do the talking and I just sit there. Occasionally they'll ask me about school or homework, but they always get the same answer. I get good grades. I behave myself. They know I'm doing okay. They know they don't have to worry too much about me.

It's Steve they need to worry about.

"And the monitor was turned off," Dad finishes. Mom starts laughing really hard. I wasn't paying any attention so I didn't get the joke. Dad looks at me as if I have three heads. "And I went all the way down there for that."

"Oh," I say. I fake laugh a little. "That's pretty funny."

He just stares at me. "Something on your mind, son?"

"What if…"

I want to do things we used to do as a family. I want us to have fun together. I remember a time when we did things that made us smile. Now it seems all Mom and Dad do is get up, go to work, come home, go to sleep, and do it all over again. The weekends are filled with chores and grocery shopping and things that really aren't that much fun to do. Everyone seems to try too hard to get along.

"What if what?"

I clear my throat then take a drink of milk. "What if we went bowling this weekend?" I ask. "We haven't been bowling in a long time."

"I have to work this weekend," Mom says. "Maybe next weekend."

"What? You work this weekend?" Dad sounds upset.

"Everyone's working overtime this week. Mandatory."

"Well," he says. "Guess it's just you and me kiddo."

"And Steve," Mom adds.

Dad clicks his tongue. "And Steve."

They don't know it but Steve is standing in the doorway. I think he was coming down to get something to eat, but I'm not sure. When he hears Dad says his name like that, he just stops. Like someone paused him or something. Then he narrows his eyes, makes a face, and quietly makes his way out of the room. I don't really think Steve would have gone to bowling with us anyway.

"Can we go see a movie?" I ask.

"I dunno," Dad teases. I know the answer is going to be yes by the way that he smiles. Then he looks at Mom. "Can he go see a horror movie?"

"Absolutely not," she says in a stern voice. She means business. "Who's gonna sit up with him when he has nightmares?"

I'm ten years old. Almost eleven. You'd think I was five by the way she talks. I'm not that scared of horror movies anymore. They still make me jump when a monster pops out but I don't pee my pants like I used to. Steve has a cool collection of horror movies on DVD, but he doesn't let me watch them very often. He says I scratch them up. That's not true. He just doesn't like other people touching his stuff.

Dad gives me a wink. "Then we'll find something more family-oriented."

That wink means he's lying.

Dad understands that I know what's going on in movies. All of my teachers say I'm smart and that I should be in a grade above what I'm in now. But Mom says that I should be treated like the other kids. Dad doesn't think so. He agrees with Ms. Embry, who is one of my all-time favorite teachers. She was my fourth grade teacher. She was really pretty and really nice. Instead of moving me up, they put me in a program called QUEST. We do some really cool things in there. But that's only for part of the day. I go to QUEST after lunch. The morning is spent with the rest of the students. Some of them throw things at me and make fun of my nose.

Mom and Dad talk about politics and the news and things they heard on talk radio while I finish my dinner. After everyone's done, I help with the dishes. I don't mind doing the dishes. Mom says it's the worst part of her day.

Dad watches sitcoms at night. I really don't like sitcoms because they pretty much tell you when to laugh. Mom doesn't like them, either. She usually reads some kind of paperback book she picked up at Wal-Mart. They're all very predictable and she likes them that way. I like horror novels by Dean Koontz and Stephen King, though I really can't get into the ones that are really long and complicated.

I go upstairs to my bedroom and play a game called *Morrowind*. It's a role-playing game for my Xbox that lets you do whatever you want. You build a character and go on journeys through this really big land and try to save it from an evil demon. I've been playing it for months now and I'm still not close to the end. Mom says that game has saved her a fortune on video games since I haven't wanted anything else since I got it.

I'm pretty much addicted to it.

Even when Mom tells me to go to bed, I wait until I think she's asleep and I start playing again. Steve likes to play, too, though he usually spends most of the time roaming the countryside in search of treasure. He doesn't play the missions like I do. Since we both have Xboxes but only one copy of the game, sometimes we fight over who's going to play. Steve always wins those fights. That's just because I don't want to become a head in his closet. I let him win.

Ten o'clock is bedtime. Mom knocks on my door even though I keep it cracked and walks in. "You know what time it is," she says. "And I don't want to hear you up after I've told you to turn that thing off." I didn't know she could hear me. I make a mental note to keep the volume turned down really low.

I turn off the Xbox and take off my clothes. I sleep in my boxers since I'm a hot sleeper. Spring nights are chilly and I like it when my covers are cold. I get under the sheets and mom turns off the light on my nightstand. Then she gives me a kiss on the forehead. She's done this since I was really little. It makes me feel safe.

"See you in the morning?" she asks.

"Of course," I say.

Just as she's about to pull the door to, I remember a question I had. "Can David spend the night Friday night?"

"We'll see," she says. This usually means yes.

"Can we order pizza?"

"I said we'll see." I decide not to push my luck.

"Can I listen to talk radio?" I ask as she pulls the door to.

"For an hour," she says. "Set it to go off in an hour."

I set my clock radio for sixty minutes and listen to a station out of Louisville. They talk about politics and entertainment and sometimes they talk about sex. Most of the stuff is over my head but it makes me feel grown-up listening to their debates. Someday I'll be on a talk radio station and I'll let everyone know how I feel. And I'll answer telephone calls from angry listeners who tell me I'm wrong.

Tonight they're talking about some sort of smoking ban. I don't know anything about that since I don't smoke. Instead of listening to that, I roll onto my back and stare at the movie posters on my ceiling. One is for *Lord Of The Rings* and the other is for *X-Men*. I'd like to write movies for a living. You get to tell a story to lots of people who will eat popcorn and tell their friends what a great movie they saw over the weekend. It's gotta be weird to see something in the theater that you once only saw in your head. I can't imagine what that feels like. I just can't.

Around midnight I get up and turn on my Xbox and watch the opening screen of *Morrowind* load up. Tonight I make sure that the volume is super low, though it does make it hard to play the game because you can't hear if there are any monsters sneaking up behind you. That's okay, though. My character is tough enough to take a few blows to the back of the head. He's a dark elf. His name is Telier.

My bedroom door opens.

Steve is standing in the doorway.

"I can see the light from your TV in the hall," he tells me. "Shut the door and stuff some clothes around the bottom."

Then he closes the door.

I get up and grab some dirty clothes. Mom will know something is up if she sees the door shut all the way, but at least it's better than letting her see the light in the hallway. I stuff the clothes across the bottom of the door. You're supposed to do this if there's ever a fire in the house. It prevents the smoke from getting in your room. Tonight it's going to help me stay out of trouble.

Steve gives me advice like that whenever he's in a good mood. That's rare, though. I guess he still wants to do the big brother thing sometimes. It's weird to get advice from a killer. It makes me wonder if I should listen to what he has to say at all. Because can you really trust a person who cuts off another person's head and stuffs it into a bowling ball bag? So far he hasn't gotten me in trouble.

I play *Morrowind* for a little while longer until it gets boring roaming the land in search of adventure and fortune. I'm also a little creeped out that Steve talked to me. It doesn't happen very often. Usually he's telling me to get out of his way or something like that. He doesn't give advice often. I'm just not used to it.

After turning off the Xbox and crawling back under the sheets, I turn the clock radio back on. The talk show I listen to has already ended. Now they're playing some sort of jazz music that I'm not familiar with. Mom and Dad listen to oldies and Steve listens to rock. My family doesn't do cool things like David's family. David's family goes to the theater to see plays and they set up homemade jewelry stands at flea markets on the weekends. Dad says they've never grown up. I don't ever want to grow up.

Ever.

Chapter 3

▼

School

I hate school.

Even though I have really bad eyesight and wear glasses my teacher makes me sit towards the back of the room. She says that I have glasses and nothing to complain about. She's wrong, though. Her name is Ms. Thomas and she's really old and ugly. Everyone calls her Crab Cake behind her back. Sometimes she makes us take notes from the overhead projector and grades us on our handwriting. I have really good handwriting so I find it easy. But I do have a hard time seeing the screen from my seat. When I asked her if I could move up front, she called my mom and told her I was a problem child. I think that's very wrong. I rarely cause any trouble in class.

Kyle Mitchell sits behind me in class. He causes all sorts of trouble. When he's not throwing paper at the back of my head or yelling out funny things during the lessons, he's rocking back and forth like he's retarded. Mom says I shouldn't say that, but it's true. He just rocks back and forth, back and forth. His eyes are blank like someone turned off his brain. Maybe someone did.

One time during math, Kyle stood up on his desk and pulled his pants down. He was wearing Superman underwear. He'd also pooped in his pants. Before Ms. Thomas could do anything, he started crying and stomping his feet on the desk. The legs came loose and the whole thing fell over. Kyle was out of school for a week after that. Ms. Thomas told us not to say anything to him about it. That didn't stop Marcus Sanders from saying anything. He makes fun of Kyle every chance he gets.

Today we're watching a video. It's about all those microscopic insects that live on your skin. There are some that even live in your eyelashes. That creeps me out. I don't like to think about creepy little insects crawling around on my skin. Last year I had a problem where I'd wash my hands all the time. I grew out of that, though.

"Pay attention," Ms. Thomas says. She's talking to me.

"Sorry," I say.

"Shhh!" She shushes me with her finger pressed against her lips.

After about half-an-hour, the video ends. Ms. Thomas turns off the television. It's almost noon.

"It's time for lunch," she tells the class. Everyone starts to get up. "I didn't say you could get up yet!"

Everyone returns to their seats.

I didn't move. I knew this was one of her tricks.

She does stuff like that all the time. She'll ask a question and if you shout out the answer without raising your hand you'll get in trouble. You have to remember that Ms. Thomas is out to get you. As long as you remember that everything she does is tricky then you'll do okay in her classroom. Steve had her when he was in elementary school. He's told me all about my teachers. He says the fifth grade is kinda tricky.

"You can get your stuff now and line up at the door," she tells us. We get up and get our stuff. My lunchbox is over near the coats with the others. It has a picture of Pokemon on the front. I just like the video games, though.

"Grow up," Kyle tells me when we get in line. He's talking about my lunchbox. "Only babies play with Pokemon."

I don't say anything. He pushes me.

"Enough!" Ms. Thomas shouts. "Get to back of the line, Kyle."

When she turns around, he flips her off.

"Kyle flipped you off!" Samantha Yields tells Ms. Thomas. Everyone turns around and starts talking.

"Be quiet!" Ms. Thomas tells us. Everyone shuts up. She walks over to Kyle and looks down at him through her thick glasses. "Did you stick up your middle finger, Kyle Mitchell?" She means business when she uses your last name.

Kyle just stares up at her. Then he sticks up his middle finger.

The class starts laughing.

I think she wants to smack him. Dad gets mad at me like that sometimes. His face turns all red and his hands turn into fists. I think one day he might punch me right in the face. I really don't know how I get him so mad so quickly. Maybe I'm not the kind of son he wanted. Instead of playing sports or doing outdoor things I draw comics and play video games in my bedroom. I also listen to talk radio.

"Fine," she says with a strange smile. "Then you can sit in here by yourself during lunch. What do you think about that, young man?"

"What?" Kyle asks. He's surprised and angry.

"I'll bring your food to you and you can sit in here and think about what you've done. And," she says with a short pause, "you can sit in here during recess and think about not being such a dirty little man anymore."

Kyle frowns. After he sits back down, he flips her off again.

The classroom laughs again.

Ms. Thomas gets everyone under control with threats and shouting. Then we're walking down the hallway towards the cafeteria. It's a long walk from our classroom because we're on the opposite end of the building. That means we have to walk through the sixth grade hallway. It's scary down there. Sometimes the kids will push you for no reason whatsoever. I hate it there.

We reach the cafeteria doors safely. Before we go inside Ms. Thomas tells the line leader to stop and puts her hands behind her back. She's going to give us a lecture. She always puts her hands behind her back when she gets after us. I guess she's supposed to look like a very important person.

"I want you all to sit at our table today," she says with a stern voice. "Nobody is going to get permission to sit at other tables."

A few kids groan.

"No exceptions!" she shouts. "Mr. Stevens says that it's getting out of hand."

Mr. Stevens is the principal. He has a cleft chin, but most of the students call it a butt chin. I bet he cries about it at night. I know I would.

"Do we have to?" Hilary Carter asks. She's blonde and pretty. Her best friends are in Mr. Yonker's class. She looks like she might cry.

"Yes," Ms. Thomas tells her. "No exceptions. I mean it."

She opens the cafeteria door and motions for the line leader to move forward. Slowly but surely the line moves inside. It's noisy and loud and there are kids everywhere. Our table is the one next to the wall near the emergency exit. Kyle likes to push it open when nobody's looking. That makes the cafeteria monitors really angry. They're all old ladies who volunteer at the school. One of them knows my Mom. I think she might be friends with my grandmother.

Those of us with lunchboxes are allowed to sit down since we don't have to wait in line for our food. They serve pizza sometimes and Mom will let me buy it when they do. She says she doesn't trust their nutritional system, though. I don't really know why she wouldn't trust them. Hundreds of kids eat their food every day and nobody's died yet. But I really don't care. Mom packs really good lunches.

I sit down at our table with about five other students. Hilary's one of them. She looks really upset and doesn't speak to me even thought she sits down across from me. I try not to look at her because that makes her mad sometimes. But she's so pretty. I've never seen someone that pretty that's not in a movie or a television show. When she's older I bet she works as an actress in Hollywood.

My lunchbox contains a thermos filled with apple juice, a dry turkey sandwich, a little bag of plain potato chips, and three chocolate chip cookies wrapped in plastic wrap. There's also an apple, but I never eat that. Mom thinks I like apples but she's wrong. I always throw the apple away. I don't know why I don't tell her I hate them.

Because we can't swap tables I can't sit with David. He's in Mr. Yonker's class, too. "This sucks," I say. Hilary narrows her eyes at me. "David is in Mr. Yonker's class and this sucks. I hate Ms. Thomas."

"It does suck," she says. She hasn't opened her lunchbox yet. "I hate this class."

"I'm sorry." I can't think of anything else to say.

"It's okay," she tells me. "I don't hate you."

I feel like my heart is going to burst. She doesn't hate me. "You don't hate me?" I ask. I always thought she did. Whenever I look at her in class she makes her face look angry and sticks her tongue out at me. If I tell her hi before homeroom she tells me to shut up. I don't understand her. I don't understand her at all.

"Of course not! You don't pick on me like Kyle does." Kyle has a big crush on Hilary, so whenever he can, he does mean things to her. Sometimes he'll pull her hair or put dirt in her lunchbox. He hasn't done anything lately.

Kyle has a short attention span. Much shorter than mine.

I look across the cafeteria at Mr. Yonker's table. David is sitting with his other friends. He has plenty of other friends. I don't have anyone else. I wave my hand hoping that he'll see me, but he just keeps talking and laughing and eating. Sitting at Mr. Yonker's table looks like fun. Sometimes I wish I was in his class instead.

"Did he see you?" Hilary asks.

"No," I tell her.

She looks over at the table, too. Her friends are also talking to their other friends. It seems as though Hilary and I have more in common than I thought. She looks at her lunchbox and begins to cry. It's the kind of crying that's silent but really painful. I do that when Dad gets angry with me.

It doesn't take long for our table to fill up. Katherine Jenkins sits beside me and talks to Hilary the whole time. She doesn't notice that Hilary's been crying. She doesn't even notice me. I take another look at Mr. Yonker's table. David has some sort of magazine he's showing to his friends. I bet it's about video games. His parents let him subscribe to all sorts of cool magazines.

I eat my lunch in silence. Hilary's conversation with Katherine is boring and dull. My food doesn't taste that good. There's something wrong with the sandwich. The meat tastes slimy and wrong. I put it back in the lunchbox so I can show Mom that there's something wrong with the meat she bought.

Forty-five minutes later, lunch is over.

We line up beside the table.

"We're going to take a bathroom break," Ms. Thomas tells the class. "So make sure you go. Nobody's going out during the lesson and that's final. Do you understand me?" Nobody says a word. "Do you understand?"

"Yes, ma'am," we all say. It sounds like everyone just woke up.

"Good," she says with a smile. Then she turns around. "Line leader, follow me." Jeffrey Perkins is the line leader. He's always been the line leader. "And stay close through the sixth grade hallway."

"Yes, ma'am," he says. But we know better than to stray.

Before too long we're back in the safety of our own hallway. The girls line up at the girl's bathroom and the boys line up at the boy's bathroom. Only five are allowed in at a time. When it's my turn, I go in with Marcus Sanders, Leroy Jackson, Randy Green, and Chris Martin. Marcus and Leroy are these two black kids who love to make jokes during lessons. They're always trying to get people to laugh. That means trouble in the bathroom. Especially when they're together.

Standing at one of the urinals with them in the room is a no-no. If you do, they'll just pull down your pants and tell everyone that you have a really small penis. It's never happened to me but I've seen it happen to many kids. Randy was one of them. It was about a month ago. He cried and called them darkies.

As soon as I go inside I make my way to a stall. That's the safest place to be. Someone has written "Eat My Shit" on the back of the door. After making sure the door is latched, I unbutton my pants and do my business. That's when someone starts banging on the door. It's probably Marcus. I'm sure Leroy's not far behind. They're like a comedy duo. Marcus is thin and has skin like a pickle while Leroy is overweight and sweats a lot. They're always telling jokes and getting in trouble.

"Open up, Martin!" Marcus laughs. "Let's see that tiny thing."

"Go away!" I shout. I push harder on my penis to make the pee come out harder and faster. "I'm trying to pee!"

"Open up, punk!" Leroy says. His fists are bigger so it sounds like an elephant beating on the door. "I'll kick your ass."

I finish peeing and put my penis back in the fly. Then I button up and move away from the door. That's when Marcus starts crawling under it, his face turned up at me. He has enormous teeth. All of them are yellow.

"He's got a tiny dick!" Marcus tells everyone.

"Come on!" I hear Ms. Thomas say from the bathroom doorway. "Don't make me have to come in there!"

"He's got a little one?" Leroy asks.

"Little bitty!" Marcus laughs. "I've never seen one so little!"

What I don't understand is that he didn't even get a good look at it. On top of that, I don't understand why he wants to know how big my penis is to begin with. I don't want people looking at my penis. When I had a physical last year, Dr. Thompson touched my testicles. His hands were cold and soft. I didn't like it then and I don't like it now.

"You guys are fags!" I tell them.

"Yeah, right," Marcus says as he crawls away.

"You are," I tell him.

Sometimes my mouth gets me into trouble.

Especially when I'm angry.

"You want to do it with me," I tell them.

"What's going on in there?" Ms. Thomas yells from the doorway.

I open the stall and face Leroy and Marcus head-on. They're both really angry that I called them fags. Marcus already has his hands balled up into fists. Leroy just puffs up his cheeks like one of those fish you see on the Discovery Channel. I know I'm going to get punched but I don't know where.

Chris and Randy are over by the sinks. Both are watching with big grins on their faces. They know I'm going to get punched, too, and they're waiting to see where I get punched. I've been in their spot before. You know someone's going to get hit when they face off like this, but the big question is where are they going to get punched. Will they cry? Will they hit back? It makes everyone tense.

"I'm coming in there!" Ms. Thomas announces. Her heels click-clock on the tile floor. "What's going on?"

Without warning, Marcus punches me in the stomach.

I throw up on his shoes.

"You fucker!" he cries. Those were his favorite pair. I've heard him talking about them in class before. His clothes may be dirty and his skin may be filthy, but he always has nice shoes. I think that's stupid.

"Marcus Albert!" she screams. "What did you do?"

"He called me a fag!" he says in defense.

"They crawled under his stall," Randy tells Ms. Thomas. "They were trying to look at his thing."

"His what?" Ms. Thomas is confused.

I wipe puke from my lips and lean against the side of the stall. It feels like the world is spinning around and around and there's nothing I can do about it. I guess I can see stars, but they really just look like little white dots.

"My penis," I manage to say. It's still hard to breathe.

"Your penis?" Ms. Thomas is now very upset. She grabs Marcus by the arm and shakes him. "Were you trying to look at his penis?"

"He said it was small," Randy tells her.

"All five of you!" she yells as her face gets redder and redder. "To the office! You'll explain yourselves to the principal."

I cough up something sticky. I hope it's not my lung.

"Are you okay?" she asks me.

"Yeah," I say as Ms. Thomas helps me to my feet.

"I'll call your mom so you can go home," she tells me as she escorts the five of us out of the bathroom. "But you have to see the principal first."

Marcus keeps jerking his arm but Ms. Thomas won't let go.

Well, at least I get to go home early.

CHAPTER 4

▼

ALONE

I get in the van and close the door.

Mom has her sad face on.

"Are you okay, honey?" she asks me as she strokes my cheek. I know I could get a toy if I wanted to, but I just want to go home. She probably has to go back to work, which means I'll be all alone.

I like being home alone during the day.

As she pulls away from the school, I start dreading tomorrow. Kids are going to know I got beat up in the bathroom. Marcus will probably tell everyone who wants to listen that I have a small penis. It's going to be brutal. My stomach starts to hurt. I'm getting gas. That happens sometimes when I'm nervous.

"Are you sure you're okay?" Mom asks at a stop sign.

"Yeah," I tell her. I'm still looking out the window. "Do you think David can spend the night?" I'm sure she'll say yes now.

I see her thinking about it. Usually you can tell what she's going to say by the expression on her face. If it's no then she'll look stern and mean. If it's yes then a smile will slowly creep across her lips. I like it when she thinks about things. That means she's taking everything into consideration. Mom says that you should always take everything into consideration. Hopefully she'll take this afternoon into consideration.

"Yes he can," she finally says. She's smiling. "But no pizza."

"Why?" We usually order pizza when David spends the night. It's a tradition.

"Because you always get gas," she explains. "And you spend half the night with a pillow in your stomach."

I sigh. She's right.

It doesn't take long for us to get home. We only live a few blocks away. When she pulls into the driveway, she checks her cell phone. I guess she's checking the time since it has a clock on the front.

"I wish I could take the rest of the day off with you," she says, "but I've gotta get back to work. I might be late tonight."

"Okay," I say.

"Have your dad fix you some leftovers."

I nod. I hate leftovers. Maybe Dad will order a pizza.

She gives me a kiss on the cheek. Her lips are dry. "Are you sure you don't want to talk about what happened today?"

I shake my head. That's the last thing I want to do. I'll have to deal with that soon enough. No sense thinking about it all day. Instead I'll play video games and hope that I can forget about it for awhile. And it's not like I'm bothered that they looked at my penis or anything because Marcus didn't even get a good look at it. It's the rumors and the jokes and the laughs that I'm worried about. It's the fact that everyone will think it's funny that Marcus saw my penis then punched me in the stomach.

"Well, call me if you need to talk, okay?" she says. I nod my head. She gives me another kiss on my cheek. "And don't answer the door."

I know not to answer the door. Sometimes they show us safety videos in school and they tell us not to answer the door if we're home alone. Kids have been kidnapped and killed because they didn't listen to their parents or the safety videos. There's no way I'm letting anyone in this house if I'm here by myself.

I get out and close the door. It closes really quietly, not like Dad's truck. Mom watches me walk all the way to the front door. She even watches me unlock the door and go inside. She doesn't start to back out until the front door is shut and she's sure that I'm not going to come back outside. I know because I watch from the window in the living room. I don't know if she sees me or not.

The van is gone in just a few seconds.

And I'm all alone.

The first thing I do is throw my backpack and my coat on Dad's recliner. Then I turn on the television and turn it up real loud so that I can hear it in the kitchen. Once I'm in the kitchen I make myself a chicken salad sandwich with a piece of cheese and Miracle Whip. It always tastes good when the house is empty. I take the bag of plain potato chips with me so I can dip them in mustard.

I watch cartoons and eat my food in the living room. Mom and Dad don't allow me to eat in the living room, but I always do when I'm alone. I have to remember to make sure that everything is clean and straight and as I found it. If I don't then they'll know and I might get grounded. They don't understand why I can't just eat in the dining room or the kitchen. I just like the living room's atmosphere. When the sun is right and the house is empty, it just feels good.

It takes three programs for me to finish eating.

Once I'm done eating, I start to get fidgety. The television isn't holding my interest any longer. I look around the living room. I get off the couch and walk to the staircase and look up at the next floor. Up there I can find stuff to do. Up there I can look at bloody things that nobody's supposed to see. Before going upstairs I check the window in case Mom came back home for some reason.

The driveway is empty.

I slowly go up the stairs. Even though nobody's home I still feel guilty for going through everyone's private things. But that doesn't stop me. I go straight for my parents room, saving my brother's severed head for last. Because after I see the head I usually don't want to snoop around anymore. I usually feel sick.

After opening the closet door, I push aside all of my mom's shoes and bags of clothes she bought but never wore. There, towards the back, is the box my dad's old cowboy boots came in. It's pretty big. Big enough for him to hide all of his dirty magazines. I crawl in and grab the box. It's heavy.

I set the box on the bed and slowly remove the top. It's been awhile since I've looked through the magazines. There's dozens of them. I usually look through the ones that have pictures of women with large breasts. There are no articles in these magazines like there are in Mom's magazines. Her magazines are about gardening and keeping your house looking very pretty.

I wonder what Dad does with these magazines. Does he look through them when nobody's home? Does Mom look at them, too? Does she care that Dad has magazines full of naked women? I think she probably would. I wonder if she knows. I'll bet she'd be really mad if she found out that Dad likes to look at naked women with large breasts. I'll have to remember that in case Dad makes me mad.

It starts to rain outside.

I feel cozy.

I spend about half-an-hour looking through the magazines. Since there's nothing to read I just flip through them after looking at the pictures. It doesn't take too long. Sometimes I wonder if Mom ever does nasty things with Dad like they do in the pictures. Does she let him put his penis in her? It seems like that would hurt. I understand some things about sex. David told me a lot but Dad says I shouldn't listen to everything David tells me. I don't know why.

After I'm done with the magazines, I put them back in order inside the box and slide them all the way towards the back of the closet. I have to make sure it looks the same so Dad doesn't suspect anything. No telling what he might do to me if he found out I knew his dark secret. Nobody likes to have their dark secrets exposed. Mom says everyone has their private things.

I guess they do.

After getting the rubber gloves from the bathroom, I walk across the hall to Steve's room. It's always cold in here. I think it's because he closes the vents so the heat from the furnace won't get in. There's always a strange smell in here. It's probably from the heads. He has a little shelf where he can burn incense, which he does whenever he's home. I think he smokes pot in there, too. Good thing Mom and Dad never come in here. They'd know something was up.

On his entertainment center is a television, Steve's Xbox, and his stereo. I push play on the stereo. Music immediately comes out of the speakers. The CD he'd been playing the night before had been on pause. There's a Joy Division case lying on his bed. Since he keeps his music in very good order, I know this is the one he's playing. He can't have two of them out of the rack at the same time. I know this from experience. When I borrowed two Nirvana albums he almost beat me up.

On his nightstand is the *Morrowind* strategy guide. This tells you how to beat the missions and gives you a map to all of the places in the game. It's cheating. I never use the strategy guide because I feel it takes away from the purpose of the game. You're supposed to explore *Morrowind*, not research it.

I notice that the closet door is only partially closed.

I open it slowly. Usually I'm hit in the face with nasty smells, but it's actually not too bad this time. I kneel down and pull the bag out of the closet. It's light. That's because it's empty. The only thing inside is some leftover blood. I zip up the bag and put it back in the closet. After pulling off the gloves, I turn off the stereo.

As I'm leaving the bedroom, I meet Steve in the hallway.

"What the fuck are you doing in my room?" he shouts. His face is red and his forehead is wrinkled. He's pissed off.

"Your door was unlocked." He shoves me against the wall.

"And that gives you permission to go inside?" he asks. His breath stinks.

"What are you doing home?" I ask.

"What are *you* doing home?" he asks.

"Some kid crawled under the stall I was in and looked at my penis. Then he punched me in the stomach."

Steve steps back. He actually looks concerned. "What?"

The storm is clearing. I decide to keep talking. "I was peeing and Marcus crawled under the stall to look at my penis. He told everyone that it was small and then he punched me in the stomach. The principal said I should go home."

"Did Mom bring you home?"

I nod. "Yeah. She was pretty upset."

He sniffs and swallows. "I'm sorry, man."

"I'm okay," I tell him. "I'm sorry for going in your room. I was just listening to a CD. I won't do it again."

He gives me a look. "It's cool. Just ask next time."

Steve heads for his bedroom.

"What are you doing home?" I ask again.

He stops before closing the door. Without turning around, he says, "I've got an appointment. I just stopped in to get something."

I don't say anything.

Steve turns around and gives me another look. I can't tell what he's thinking. "Which Marcus was it?"

"Marcus Sanders," I say.

Without saying another word, he goes into his bedroom and closes the door. I stand in the hallway, the rubber gloves still hidden behind my back. Why did he want to know about Marcus? I start to think about the horrible things my brother might do to Marcus. What if he cut off his head? What if I came home and found him in the bowling ball bag? Would I laugh or would I cry?

I go into my bedroom and shut the door.

It doesn't take me long to fall asleep after I lay down on the bed.

As I doze, I wonder what he did with the head.

What does he do with the heads?

CHAPTER 5

▼

EVENTFUL

Turns out Mom didn't have to work late after all.

She tells Dad what happened during dinner.

"He did what?" Dad says. Food hangs from his fork.

"He crawled under the stall and looked at my penis. Then he punched me in the stomach," I tell him. He still hasn't taken his bite yet. I can see the redness creeping up his neck. Everyone in my family turns bright red when they get upset, but Dad gets really red. Mom calls it his "tomato face."

"And what happened to this little pervert who hit you?" he asks.

"Suspended for a week," she explains before taking a drink of unsweetened tea. After swallowing, she says, "Parents couldn't have cared less."

"Great," Dad says with his mouth full. "Another degenerate nigger."

Mom's eyes widen.

"Sorry," he says. "I didn't mean that."

Dad's got a mean streak in him. I don't know why, but he's never been really friendly towards black people. He doesn't think they should go back to Africa or anything but he thinks they should keep to themselves. He also hates it when black people date white people. If he sees a black and white couple in a movie he starts mouthing off about how it's not right. I never want to act that way towards other people. There's no sense in getting angry over stupid stuff.

Mom gives him the you-should-know-better face and says to me, "If you want, you can stay home from school tomorrow."

I stop chewing.

Dad stops chewing, too.

"Really?" I say. I can't believe it.

She looks at Dad. Dad shrugs and makes a weird face. It's his you-know-what's-best face. "You can stay home and I'll rent you two movies," she says. "You've had a rough day. Nobody should have to go through that."

"What about David?" I ask.

She just looks at me. "What *about* David?"

"Can he still spend the night?"

Her eyes close. She's forgotten about the sleepover.

"Can he?" I ask.

"It's fine with me," Dad finally says after several seconds of nothing. "If it's okay with your mother, I mean."

"I told you he could," she says. And that's it.

She starts eating again.

Dad and I look at each other. He gives me a little smile.

"When can we go to the video store?" I ask.

"After dinner," Mom says with a mouth full of food.

I take a bite. "Can I call David and let him know about the sleepover?"

"After we get back," she tells me. "Stop with the questions already."

I don't ask anything else, but that doesn't mean I don't have questions. I need to ask about the pizza again. I need to ask if we can rent two additional videos tomorrow night since I'm getting two tonight. And I need to ask if I can rent horror movies. She'll probably get upset if I ask now, so I don't say anything else. Asking at the video store might be better. It might catch her by surprise.

Mom and Dad talk about news and stuff for the rest of dinner. I eat in silence, thinking about what I'm going to rent at the video store. I have to rent on VHS because I don't have a DVD player in my bedroom. That's in the living room. The only reason I want to leave my bedroom tomorrow is to use the bathroom. I plan on bringing in the two-liter of Coke and several bags of chips so I don't have to get up for anything. I'm going to enjoy myself for a change.

I think I've earned it.

After dinner I help with the dishes. Since I'm a very slow washer, Mom always makes me dry. Dad goes into the living room and starts flipping through the channels, trying to find what he wants to watch tonight. Mom doesn't really talk too much. She seems to have a lot on her mind. Her job is stressful, she says, and I think that makes her cranky and tired. I don't want a job that makes me cranky and tired.

Just as we're finishing, Steve walks through the back door.

He looks like he's ready to explode.

Mom notices his mood and doesn't say anything. She doesn't even move. I wave at him as he walks by. He stops right in front of me and looks down. It's like he doesn't even know me. Like I'm just some stupid kid that helps his mom dry the dishes every night. I can't describe how it makes me feel.

"Did you go in my room again?" he asks.

"No," I say.

"You sure?"

I nod.

"What?" he asks. His eyes are narrow and mean.

"I'm sure, Steve. I told you I wouldn't."

He points his finger at me. "Make sure you don't. And I'm keeping the door locked from now on. You got that?"

Then he's gone.

We hear him walk up the stairs.

After a few seconds, Mom asks, "You went into his room? Are you crazy?"

"I wanted to listen to a CD," I say. It's the same lie I told Steve.

"Well, you've got a death wish if you go in there," she warns me. I already know this. "I'm only telling you this once, okay?"

"Okay," I say. I'm looking at the floor.

"Look at me."

I look at her eyes. They're stern and mean. "Do not go into your brother's room, okay? He pays rent. He has a right to his privacy."

"I got it," I tell her. I want to cry but I don't. I hate getting scolded.

We finish the dishes in silence.

After everything is wiped down and put away, Mom gets her purse from the bedroom. "Get your coat," she tells me. "It's a little cold outside."

The video store. I almost forgot about that.

It doesn't take long for me to get my things together so we can go. I climb into the passenger side of our mini-van and buckle up. Mom won't move the van if I'm not buckled in, so that's always the first thing I do. Once she gets inside, she starts the engine and turns on the heat. It's really cold out tonight. Colder than it was last night, which is really saying something.

"Can we listen to the radio?" I ask.

"Yes," she says. "But no rap."

I turn on the radio and change the channel.

The video store is about ten minutes away. Because of the traffic, it takes us longer to get there. Mom says some not-so-bad words about the timing of the traffic lights and rolls down her window to get some fresh air. I listen to the radio and prepare myself to ask her about the horror movies. Hopefully she won't be in a bad mood and say no. I'm really in the mood for something scary.

Just as she's about to turn into the shopping center where the video store's at, someone in a green car with tinted windows cuts her off. She has to turn the wheel really hard to avoid hitting them, causing us to bump against the curb. The brakes make really loud noises as she tries to stop us from going into the grass. Someone behind us honks their horn. Mom says some really dirty words and sticks up her middle finger at the rear view mirror. She's not a very friendly driver.

Finally, we come to a stop in the turn lane.

Mom turns on the emergency lights.

"Are you okay?" she asks. She's out of breath.

"I'm okay," I tell her. "Promise."

She takes in a deep breath. "It's been a rough day."

"Yeah, it has."

Mom looks at me as if I'm the saddest thing she's ever seen. She unbuckles her seat belt and gives me a hug. Her tears fall on my neck. She doesn't try to clean them up. She doesn't try to do anything. She just sits there and hugs me. A car pulls up beside us and the driver motions for my mom to roll down her window. After wiping away the tears, she quickly rolls it down.

"Are you okay?" a man with glasses asks.

"We're okay," she tells him. "Just a little frazzled, that's all."

"Do I need to call anyone?" He holds up a tiny cell phone. It looks like the one Dad carries. I like the sound it makes when it rings.

"We're okay," she tells him again. Now she sounds a little irritated. "Like I said, we're just a little shaken up."

"Well, I'll be in the grocery store if you need anything," he tells her with a wink. "Just come get me."

Mom rolls up her window really fast.

The man with glasses drives off.

I feel really strange. Almost as strange as when Marcus crawled under the stall to look at me. Mom puts her hands on the steering wheel and looks in the rear view mirror. After giving me a sad smile, she puts the van back into gear and turns off the emergency lights. I guess everything's okay.

She pulls into the parking lot and turns off the van.

"If that man comes into the video store," Mom says, "we're going home, okay? I don't think we can trust him."

"Me, neither," I say. "He seemed creepy."

Mom messes up her face. "I know, right?"

We laugh at the man with glasses. It's a nervous laugh.

"Are you ready?" she asks.

I nod and smile.

"Let's go." She opens her door and gets out. I do the same.

The wind is blowing as we walk across the parking lot. I think my lips are getting chapped. I keep licking them anyway because I hate the feeling of dry lips. As we get closer to the store I can start to make out posters in the window. Most of them are for movies that I really don't want to see. Movies that are about women and their problems or married people and their problems. Maybe it's because I really don't know much about that stuff. Maybe I'm just too young.

When you first get inside the video store, you have to walk down a little hallway that's covered with movie posters. None of them look good, either. After the hallway is the store, which is a huge room lit with really dirty ceiling lights. They make everything look yellow. The carpet is yellow, too. The shelves are black and dusty and crammed with movies. There's always a strange smell in here, too. It smells like burnt popcorn and really old socks. Nowhere else smells like this place.

The new releases wrap all around the walls. Towards the very back of the store is the adult room. I've never been inside, but I've had dreams where I open the door and go in. The videos inside are really scary and gross. These dreams almost always turn into nightmares because I try not to look at the really disturbing pictures on the boxes. It's been a while since I've had a dream like this, though.

The guy behind the counter is a skinny white guy named Hank. He usually works during the night, which is when Mom normally takes me. When he sees us walk up the hallway he smiles and waves. I wave back. It's nice when someone recognizes you like that. It makes me feel special.

"Pick out two movies," Mom tells me.

I look at the horror section. "Mom?"

"Yeah?" She's looking at the new release section.

I take in a deep breath and prepare myself.

"Can I rent a horror movie?"

She doesn't say anything.

"Can I rent a horror movie?" I ask again.

She lets out a sigh. "Promise you won't get too scared?"

I can't promise that, but I do anyway.

"Okay," she tells me. "But nothing too gross."

I can't help but smile.

But that wasn't the hard part.

The hard part is actually picking out what movies I want to rent. The horror section in this video store is really big, so I have lots of choices to choose from. I walk down the aisle slowly, looking over the different pictures on the front of the boxes. Which ones should I get? Which ones look scary?

Occasionally I'll look over my shoulder at Mom. She's looking at the new releases. That's all they ever rent. Usually Dad falls asleep during the movie and Mom watches it by herself. We spend so much time in this video store that I'm surprised she can find anything she hasn't seen yet. I get my love of movies from my mom. Dad likes sitcoms and weekend sports shows.

I've seen a lot of horror movies from this video store. Every so often they'll add a few old movies. There's one called *Street Trash* that I've never seen in here before. I pick it up and quickly look over my shoulder. I keep expecting Mom to say something about what I've picked out, but she's too busy with the new releases. I continue down the horror aisle, looking at each box individually and saying the title two or three times in my head before moving on. It's just something I do.

Towards the end of the aisle, I spot something familiar.

The name of the movie is *Headless*, and it stars some guy I've never seen before. On the box is a picture of a man dressed in all black with large, silver balls where his eyes should be. His mouth is open in a scream. His face and clothes are drenched in blood. In one hand is a machete and in the other is a severed head. The eyes have been gouged out and its tongue hangs from its mouth.

I almost drop my movie in shock.

I've seen this before. Only it was in my brother's bedroom closet, tucked away from the world inside a sticky, smelly bowling ball bag.

The movie's checked out, though.

I put this one on my mental list of movies I need to see. That list keeps growing and growing, but I'm sure I'll see them all one day. The only reason I want to see it is because it reminds me of what Steve does in his spare time. Has he seen this movie? Is he trying to imitate what he saw? Ms. Donaldson, my QUEST teacher, thinks that violence in movies and video games are making kids more violent. Mom says the exact same thing. I don't think so. I watch violent movies and play violent video games all the time and I get beat up without even hitting back.

The other movie I decide to get is *Hellraiser*. I've seen this movie before but it's really scary and really gross. This one parts shows a guy's dead body growing out of a floor in this really old house. Hopefully Mom won't go back and check what movies I picked out. She hasn't done this in a long time so I'm hoping that's something she's not going to do anymore. I'm older now, anyway.

Since I have my two movies, I go back to where Mom is. She's still looking through the new releases. Under her arm is one movie, but I can't see what it is because of the way she's holding the tape. I'll bet it's something I wouldn't like. I don't usually like the movies my parents watch.

"Did you find anything?" she asks.

"Yeah," I say. I smile when I say it.

"What did you get?"

I clear my throat. "I got *Hellraiser* and *Street Trash*."

Mom looks at me. "There's actually a movie called *Street Trash*?"

"Yeah," I tell her. I hold up the video. "See?"

She just looks at me. "And you want to see this?"

She's making me nervous.

"Yeah," I say. "What's wrong with that?"

Mom closes her eyes and shakes her head. "You're a weird boy."

I don't know what she means. Is she being serious or is she just pulling my leg? Because if she's serious then she's no better than the kids at school who call me names. Even though she may have said it nicer it still doesn't mean she should say it. But Mom jokes around sometimes. I can't tell if she's joking or not.

I just smile and shrug.

"Well, I think I've got what I want," she tells me. "We can go if you're ready."

"I'm ready," I say.

We walk to the front of the store.

Hanks nods as we put our movies on the counter. Mom gets her membership card out of her purse and hands it to him. He scans the back of it using a hand-held scanner and gives it back. After pressing a few buttons on the keyboard, he begins scanning each movie. Then he tells us how much we owe him.

Mom hands him the money.

"Can you look up a movie?" I ask.

Mom gives me a look. It's her don't-embarrass-me face.

"Sure," he says. "Whatcha got in mind?"

"A movie called *Headless*," I tell him. "It's a horror movie."

Mom seems uncomfortable. I think I might be embarrassing her.

Hank types something on the keyboard and looks at the computer screen. "It's not back there?" he asks.

"Nope," I tell him. "It's not behind the box."

"This thing hasn't rented in months," he says. "If it's not back there then I don't know where it is."

"Did someone steal it?" I ask.

"Marty," Mom says with a nervous laugh. "Come on."

"I dunno," Hank says as he shrugs his shoulders. "If it's not behind the box then it's either misplaced or stolen. Sorry."

"Thanks," I tell him.

We walk through the alarm system and Mom takes the bag of movies. You can't walk through the alarm system with the movies or it will go off. I've heard it go off before and it's really, really loud and annoying. This is to keep people from stealing movies. I guess it doesn't work that well.

As we leave the video store, Mom asks, "Asking about movies now, are we?"

"I was just wondering," I tell her.

"My little man," she says. She messes up my hair and laughs.

Nothing happens on the way home.

And that's fine with me.

CHAPTER 6

▼

CONVERSATIONS

In the living room, I hear Mom tell Dad about our little accident.

He doesn't seem too worried about it.

She doesn't tell him about the man with the glasses.

I sit in the kitchen with the lights out. The only thing that's giving off any light is the moon and that's coming through the window. I sit on the counter because this is where I sit when I talk on the telephone. Since I'm really not allowed in my parents room, this is the only other place I can go.

I dial David's number and wait for someone to pick up.

"Hello?" It's David's mother. I don't know her name.

"Is David there?" I ask. I always ask that when I call someone. Instead of asking if I can speak to them, I just ask if they are at home.

"May I ask who's calling?" she asks. She sounds snotty.

"It's Marty," I tell her.

She doesn't say anything else. I hear her set the phone down.

"David!" she screams. "Telephone!"

I hear David's footsteps as he runs down their wooden staircase.

He picks up the phone. "Hello?"

"Hey," I say. "It's Marty."

"Hey," he says. "What's up?"

"My mom says you can spend the night Friday," I tell him. "She said it's cool if you want to." I clear my throat. "Do you?"

"I guess," he says. He doesn't sound too excited about it, though. I wonder why he doesn't? "I've gotta ask my mom, though. I'm sure she'll say yes. She's always looking for ways to get me outta the house." That's the truth. Whenever I go over to David's house, she always makes us play outside. I like playing outside sometimes, but I have more fun doing things inside.

"Go ask," I say. "Then come tell me, okay?"

"Hold on." David sets down the phone and walks off. I can't hear anything he says. All I can hear is their television. Someone's watching *Friends*. I can't tell what episode because it's not that loud.

It takes David a few minutes to get back to the phone. That usually means bad news. But David just doesn't take no for an answer. If someone tells him no then he whines and complains until things start to go his way. Dad says that David is spoiled because he's an only child. But Dad says a lot of bad things about a lot of good people. Sometimes it's hard to listen to him talk.

David picks up the phone. "Still there?"

"Yeah." I'm nervous.

"She said I could," he says. He still doesn't sound excited. "But I gotta be home by noon on Saturday. Is that okay?"

"That's cool," I tell him.

Then everything goes silent.

"Are they talking about me at school?" I finally ask him. I really don't want to know. I don't want to know what they're saying.

That's a lie. I really do care about what they're saying.

"A little," David says. "You know how Marcus is."

"So you heard?"

"Yeah," he tells me. "Marcus told everyone at recess that you have a really small dick and he beat the shit out of you in the bathroom for trying to kiss him."

I get a sinking feeling in my belly.

It's worse than I thought.

"He said I tried to kiss him?" I ask. I can't believe what I'm hearing.

"Yeah," David tells me. "Leroy was sayin' it, too. Both of them were goin' all over the playground. They told it to everyone."

I want to lay down and sleep until it all goes away. Not only are they spreading rumors about my penis and telling everyone that Marcus beat me up, but they're lying about me trying to kiss him. I'd never try to kiss Marcus or Leroy. He's a liar and that makes me very angry.

"You still there?" David asks.

"Yeah," I say. I take in a breath and sigh. "I can't believe they're saying that."

"You know Marcus," he says again. "He's a dickhole."

I want to throw up. I want to run away. I want to go to a school where everyone is nice and peaceful and the students don't make up nasty rumors about you during recess. I want to eat lunch with my friends and not be bothered. I want to do my homework and not get made fun of because I actually did it and turned it in. I just want to be left alone so I can be who I am without people laughing.

"I just can't believe it," is all I can say. I'm out of words.

"Are you coming to school tomorrow?" he asks.

"No," I tell him. "Mom says I can take the day off."

"Lucky fuck," he says as he laughs. "I wish someone would make fun of my dick so I could stay at home all day."

I laugh, too, even though it's really not that funny.

David changes the subject. "What time do you want me to come over?"

"As soon as you can," I tell him. "After school?"

"I gotta stop back home to pick up my clothes and shit, but I can come over after school if you want me to," he explains. "Do you want me to bring anything?"

I think about it for a second. David has a Playstation 2 with some really cool games. He also has a big collection of Japanese comic books that make the violence in my comic books look very weak. He also has a really cool MP3 player that he keeps loaded with new albums that he downloads off the Internet. David has so much cool stuff that I really don't know where to start.

"I guess bring your MP3 player and your comics," I tell him. "Maybe we could work on the comic book tomorrow."

"Cool," he says. He likes that idea. I can hear it in his voice. "We can listen to my MP3 player and draw shit."

"Yeah," I say. I'm smiling, too. "We can watch some horror movies, too."

"Really? Your mom's cool with that?"

"We can watch them in my room," I explain without really answering his question. "With the lights out so it's scary."

David laughs. "It's gonna be cool."

We talk for a little while longer about what we're going to do, but it's nothing really important. After I hang up the phone, I get off the counter and pet my Dad's cat. His name is Tubby. The reason I say it's Dad's cat is because he's usually the only person it deals with. My mom can't stand the cat and gets mad when she has to clean cat hair off the furniture. Dad loves the fluffy thing to death.

"Are you off the phone?" Mom shouts from the living room.

"Yeah!" I shout back.

"I'm gonna call Mom," she says, though I'm not sure who she's talking to. I hear her climb the stairs. She's going to call from her bedroom.

I open the cabinet and take out a box of Cheese Nips. After opening the box and the plastic bag inside, I pull out a handful of crackers and stuff them in my mouth. I chew it until it's nothing but cheesy paste in my mouth. Then I work it around with my tongue until all the flavor is gone. I have to bite the wad of crackers in half so I won't choke when I swallow. One time I almost choked on it.

I walk into the living room. Dad doesn't look up.

"What are you watching?" I ask.

Dad mumbles something and shifts in his seat. It looks like some sort of cop show. This one is an hour long and deals with the cops and the lawyers. I'm not sure what it's called, but he likes it just as much as his sitcoms. I should know better than to bother him during his cop show, but I do it anyway. Sometimes I just like to annoy him. I really don't know why. It makes me feel better, I guess.

"I'm going upstairs," I tell him.

Dad says nothing.

I climb the stairs two at a time. That way it doesn't take me very long to get to the second floor. Steve's door is closed and I can hear music coming from inside. That means you shouldn't bother him. When the music's playing, he says, you should stay away. I think about annoying him, too, but I don't want him to beat me up. That's already happened once today. I can't take too much more.

Mom's in her bedroom talking to my grandmother. Her mom. My grandmother is a really nice person. Whenever I go over to her apartment on the other side of town she gives me candy. She's got a bird that can say things like "kissy kissy" and "I'm a pretty bird." It's really freaky. I stand in the hallway and listen to their conversation for a minute. They're talking about work and the news and stuff they've seen on TV. Then I go into my bedroom and close the door.

On my bed are the two movies I rented. I want to watch one of them tonight. If I do that, I'll only have one to watch tomorrow when everyone's gone. I pick up *Hellraiser* and look at the label on the cassette. It's worn and looks like it's ready to come off. I wonder how long this one's been on the shelves? How many people have watched it? I know I've rented it at least three times already.

I decide to save both movies for tomorrow. It's a good idea.

The rest of the night is pretty much spent playing *Morrowind*. I really don't think too much about the game while I'm playing it. I start thinking about school and what Marcus did. I think about what David told me about everyone knowing what happened. My belly starts to hurt. I don't like to think about stuff like this. Mom says it's the tension in my belly that makes it hurt. I don't know what causes it, but it sure does hurt.

Mom knocks on my door.

"It's lights out, kiddo," she says.

"But I don't have to go to school tomorrow," I tell her. "Why should I go to bed early when I don't have to get up early?"

"Because," she says. She's standing in my room now, watching me play *Morrowind*. "Because it's bedtime."

Everyone has the same bedtime in our house. Except Steve. He does what he wants whenever he wants to. I go to bed at ten and Mom and Dad go to bed between ten and eleven. Sometimes they stay up later, watching the news while they get ready for bed. I don't know why it takes so long for them to get ready for bed. All I do is slide under the covers and close my eyes.

"But I want to play," I say. I'm whining. She hates it when I whine.

"Enough," she says. "Save your game."

I go to the main menu and save my game. After the little box that says "Saving Game—Do Not Turn Off Your Xbox" disappears, Mom turns off the TV. I crawl under the covers and turn on my clock radio. It's already set for one hour. I tell Mom I've already got it set. She gives me a look.

"Who said you could listen to it?" she asks. Her eyes are like slits. I think she might be joking, but I can't really tell.

"You usually say yes," I say.

Mom smiles. "You can listen to it." She sits down on the edge of my bed and runs her fingers through my hair. "Are you okay?"

I look at the foot of my bed. "I'm okay," I tell her.

I'm lying. She knows it, too.

"If you want to talk, all you have to do is come find me," she tells me. "I want you to talk to me if anything's bothering you."

"I know," I say. I don't want to talk about this anymore. It's all I can think about. I just want to forget about it for a while.

We're quiet for a moment.

"Thanks for not making me go to school tomorrow," I tell her. I try to smile but my lips don't want to work. "David said everyone knows."

Mom messes up my hair. "Well, don't worry about that tomorrow, okay? You've got two movies and the house to yourself."

I like the way she makes things so simple. Moms sometimes have a way of making things okay. If I'm having a really bad day, then all I have to do is tell

Mom about it. She has a way of "putting things into perspective." That's what she calls it. I think all Moms probably can do this. At least they should try.

"Well, thanks anyway," I tell her.

"You're welcome." She kisses me on the forehead.

We tell each other goodnight and she turns out the light.

Just as she's about to close the door, she stops. "There's a chance of a storm tonight," she tells me.

"Really?" I like storms at night.

"Yeah," she says. "Thought you might like that."

She pulls the door until it's open just a crack. Then she's gone. I can hear her talking to my dad in the other room. Their voices are too low for me to really hear what they're talking about. A soft thumping sound is coming from Steve's room. He's still listening to music. It seems like he's always listening to something. I wonder if he listens to music when he's killing people?

I fall asleep before my clock radio turns itself off.

And everything is quiet.

Until the storm.

CHAPTER 7

▼

STORM

Thunder wakes me up.

It's loud. Really, really loud. And dark. Really, really dark. That means the electricity probably went out. Whenever there's a bad storm our lights almost always go out. Dad says it's because we live in a crappy neighborhood. Mom says it's because the storms around here are just really strong. I don't know who's right or wrong about our electricity, but the storms we get are usually bad. I don't mind, though. I like watching the lightning through my bedroom window.

But tonight's storm feels different.

It's louder than normal. And the lightning flashes are fast and they happen a lot. The wind blows rain against my window. I'm afraid that the glass might shatter and make a big mess. If that happened, the glass would blow right onto my bed and cut me to shreds. The blood would make everything sticky.

Since my clock radio isn't working, I don't know what time it is. I get out of bed and walk over to my dresser. Using my hands, I try to find my watch in the dark. It has a button you can push that lights up the display. That way I can find out what time it is. The only thing I do while searching for my watch is knock lots of stuff onto the floor. If I wake up my parents, I'll be in big trouble. Dad gets upset if you wake him up because he has such a hard time falling asleep to begin with.

Finally I find my watch. The display says it's two-thirty-two. It's still pretty early. As I'm crawling back into bed, a huge lightning flash lights up my bedroom. Thunder booms a second later. That means it struck nearby, which is pretty scary. I want a flashlight. I need a flashlight. If a branch or something comes through my window I want to be able to see how to get out of my room. And since the electricity is out, I won't be able to see without a flashlight.

I have a flashlight, but I took the batteries from it and put them in my remote-controlled car. I race it up and down the driveway sometimes. Mom says it makes too much noise but it's really not that bad. But I left the remote control on all night and ran down the batteries. Now I don't have any. That means I'll have to ask either Mom and Dad or Steve for a flashlight. Tough decision.

I open my bedroom door and creep into the hallway.

I've always been afraid of our hallway. Sometimes I have nightmares about this hallway. In these dreams I'm trying to go to the bathroom but something grabs my legs and slowly pulls me into the darkness. I'm afraid to look behind me to see what it is. Whenever there's a monster in my dreams I never look at it. My imagination is so crazy that there's no telling what they might look like.

Sometimes my parents don't close their door all the way. I can see them sleeping. Even if I couldn't see them I can hear them both snoring. Loudly. Waking up my parents for something in the middle of the night isn't a good idea. Both of them get grumpy because they have to get up early for work. So if there's something I need in the middle of the night, I usually ask Steve first. If he says no or doesn't answer his door, then I go to them. Steve is usually pretty good about helping me out. Sometimes he's in a bad mood and he'll yell at me. I'm getting used to it, though.

Things weren't always so bad between Steve and everyone. We used to watch TV together at night. We used to laugh and go do things during the summer. We used to rent movies and pop popcorn on the stove. We were a family. Then one day it all changed, like someone had switched Steve's brain with someone else's. He just stopped doing everything. And everything fell apart. No more trips to the lake. No more trips to really cool places around Kentucky. No more family time.

I really don't think he knows how much he's hurting everyone.

Steve's door is closed. I knock on it.

No answer.

I knock again. He doesn't open it.

"Steve?" I whisper, though it's pretty loud. "Are you awake?"

He doesn't say anything.

"I need a flashlight," I tell him. "You got one?"

Thunder booms outside. He doesn't answer me.

I knock on his door and take a step back. If he is asleep, then he'll be mad that I woke him up. That means he'll open the door really fast and stick out his head. After he sees who woke him up, he'll start yelling. And when Steve yells at you, you want to be as far away as possible. He spits really bad when he yells and his breath is bad because he doesn't brush his teeth everyday. It's true.

But nothing happens when I knock.

No yelling. No screaming. No waking up my parents with his ranting and raving. No punishment for bothering my brother. No problems. All I hear is the rainstorm outside. Even though I know better than to meddle in other people things, I try the doorknob to see if it's locked. It is. That lock is useless, though. All you need is a butter knife to pop the lock. I've done it to my bedroom door when I accidentally locked myself out one time. I don't play with the locks anymore.

"Steve?" I ask one more time. I have to be sure he's not in there if I break into his room. No telling what might happen if he caught me doing that.

It's true when I say that I know better than to do some of the stuff I do. I know it's wrong to go downstairs to get a butter knife. But I do it anyway. I know it's wrong to pop the lock and sneak into my brother's room to get a flashlight. But I do it anyway. I ease the door open, slide inside, and close it back gently. Our doors can be noisy sometimes. Once I'm inside, I find out why he didn't answer.

It's because he's not there.

Everything's dark. Completely dark. I'm not sure it's really empty or not until a flash of lightning lets me get a good look for just a second. Everything looks okay. I walk really carefully across his floor. We have hardwood floors in our house and sometimes they creak really loud. Sometimes it'll wake you up if you're not really sound asleep. I don't want to wake up my parents. Getting caught in here by them might be worse than getting caught by Steve. Dad would yell his head off.

He keeps his flashlight in the nightstand next to his bed. I know this because I'm a big snoop and I can't keep my nose out of other people's business. But it really helps to know all this stuff when you're looking for a flashlight in a thunderstorm. He also keeps a bag of gummy bears, band aids, some playing cards, and a few small candles in there. The flashlight is towards the very back, so I have to be sure I don't knock anything over and wake up my parents. That's very important.

I finally get the flashlight out and turn it on to make sure it works.

That's when I hear the window opening.

I quickly turn off the flashlight. Did he see me?

I can't take any chances.

Since it's dark in the room, Steve really can't see what's going on. I roll under his bed, taking the flashlight with me. I'm careful not to make too much noise. He closes the window and clears his throat. Every part of me is tingling. I'm scared to death. The one thing that I prayed wouldn't happen has actually happened. This proves that God just doesn't seem to like me. But I guess this is what I get for not being a good boy and doing what I'm told. I should've done what I was told.

"What the fuck?" he whispers to himself. "I thought I left those goddamn lights on?" Steve is known for talking to himself. My grandmother used to tell me that if you talked to yourself then you were probably crazy.

He slowly makes his way over to the light switch. I know this because I can hear him try it again and again and again. "Fuck," he says. It's in a low voice but it's harsh and angry. "Why the fuck does the power gotta go out tonight, huh? Because I fucking need to find something, that's why."

All I can really see are his feet, and I can't even see them that well. I can see that he's dripping water all over the floor, though. Mom would have a fit. Anyway, my eyes have adjusted to the darkness a little bit, but it's still hard to make out shapes. If I squint my eyes and try real hard, I can kinda make out what shoes he's got on. It looks like he's wearing those combat boots he keeps in his closet. The ones with the steel spikes going up the sides. I guess he thinks that's cool.

Steve walks to the end of his bed. I'm face-to-face with the back of his combat boots. In front of him is the closet door. He slowly opens the squeaky metal doors and begins to search around the closet for something. Judging from how hard he's huffing and puffing, he must not be having a very good time doing it. A few more bad words fly out of his mouth. They're louder this time.

"What the fuck?" he asks. "Where the fuck is it?"

Something falls out of the closet and lands on the hardwood floor. It's pretty loud. I stop breathing immediately. Steve stops moving. All I can hear is the rain outside and a little bit of thunder. Nothing else. It's so quiet that my ears are buzzing.

Then, all of a sudden, Steve starts digging frantically through his closet. Clothes are being knocked down from the hangers. Things are getting pretty messy. He even gets down on his hands and knees and begins digging through the junk on the floor. It reminds me of Mom working in her garden. After a few minutes of searching, he stands up. I can hear him mumbling but I can't really hear what he's saying. I'll bet he's standing in front of the closet with a blank expression on his face. I'll bet he's got a hand on his head, picking at his scalp like he always does when he's upset.

Steve starts to look through the rest of the room. And it dawns on me. What if he looks under the bed? What if he gets down on his hands and knees and takes a look at what's under his bed? What would I say? What would I do? My heart won't stop pounding. I'm afraid he'll hear it and find out that I popped the lock and snuck into his bedroom. There's no telling what would happen then. He might even get mad enough to kill me. I hope I never see him that angry.

He stops moving again. I can hear him huffing

"Fuck," he says. "What the fuck did I do with it?"

He goes back to the closet and stops moving. He's probably thinking about the last place he saw it. Maybe he last saw it on the bed. Maybe it got knocked off by accident before he left. Maybe it rolled under the bed. Maybe I'm as good as dead. Maybe I'm taking my last breath right now.

I hear him open a dresser drawer. More things hit the floor. I'm surprised Dad hasn't shouted something yet. The rain must be covering up the noise Steve's making. "Aha!" he says. He quickly shuts the drawer and walks to the front of the closet. He doesn't say anything. All I can hear is him breathing.

I wonder what he was looking for? Is it a weapon? Something used to remove people's eyes? Something used to remove people's tongues? Something used to torture people? I've really seen too many horror movies because I have tons of ideas and all of them are pretty gross. It could be his car keys or his wallet or something simple like that. It doesn't have to be something scary.

But knowing Steve, it probably is.

"Are you ready?" he asks. He's talking to himself again. I'll bet he's looking in the mirror, too. "Can you handle this?"

"I can handle this," he says. His voice is different. Like he's trying to sound really mean and evil. He's not doing a very good job. "I can handle anything."

"Can you?" He sounds like Steve again.

"I can handle anything," says the evil voice. "Anything you got."

Then he laughs.

And it's the scariest sound I've ever heard.

It's the kind of laugh you know is coming from something or someone that's really mean. Someone that's truly evil. Someone that will probably come back from the dead two or three times after you think you've finally killed him. But the laughter doesn't sound corny or anything. It sounds like the real laughter that a real madman might make right before he cuts the head off some poor black woman who keeps screaming for help even after the head's been completely removed. What if he knows I'm under the bed? Maybe I'm the punch line to his joke.

I close my eyes and bite my tongue really hard.

These thoughts keep coming back into my head. I keep seeing him throwing the mattress across the room as he makes his way towards my secret hiding space. He's probably have a machete that's covered in blood in his right hand. He might even have other weapons attached to his belt. And there's no telling what kind of mask he's wearing. All good serial killers wear masks, so I know he's probably got one, too. I can't keep these thoughts from taking over.

My breathing keeps getting faster.

I'm shaking all over.

I'm sweating.

Mom calls these panic attacks.

I'm overwhelmed with fear. I'm going to die. I want to crawl under the table and turn off all the lights so that I can be completely alone. I need to be alone. I close my eyes tighter and bite my tongue harder. Anything to keep the complete and utter terror from taking control of my brain. If it takes over control, I'm a goner.

I hear him open the window and I start to calm down. He's leaving. I'm safe. I watch his feet disappear off the ground. The window is closed and Steve is gone. I am all alone. My breathing begins to slow down. I don't feel like the world is coming to an end anymore. My thoughts are no longer jumbled.

I'm returning to normal.

It's still raining outside. It's a good sound.

Back in my bedroom, I hide beneath the sheets. I can only think about Steve. Why was he going out there tonight? Who was he with? Was he going to kill her? Was he going to cut off her head and keep it stashed in the closet for a week or two? And what does he do with the heads? Does he look at them? Study them? I want to know the answers to these questions. I need to understand my big brother.

Because I need to understand what I might be up against.

But it's getting late and I'm sleepy.

I stick the flashlight beneath my pillow and snuggle deep beneath the covers.

Listening to the rain outside puts me to sleep.

CHAPTER 8

▼

VACATION

When I finally wake up, the clock is blinking.

Mom and Dad didn't wake me up before they left. Usually, if I'm home alone, they wake me up before they leave just so I'll know that I'm going to be home alone. Sometimes I don't like to be left alone all day. Sometimes the house just seems too big and too empty. Not today, though. I'm excited that I have the day off. I don't have to face the kids at school after what Marcus did. Maybe everyone will forget over the weekend. Probably not, though. I'm never that lucky. Knowing my luck they'll have a nickname for me on Monday. I'm doomed.

I try not to think about school. If I think about that too much then I know I'll end up in a bad mood. I'll get all upset about Marcus and end up spending the day in bed. If I'm having a bad day and I'm home alone, I usually spend the entire time trying to sleep. Sleeping helps me forget about the horrible things that happen in my life. Dreams are relaxing most of the time. Dad says that relaxation is important. That's why he likes to sit around and watch sports on the weekends.

After lying in bed for a little while, I finally crawl out and head to the bathroom. It feels like my bladder is about to explode. I use my little penis to pee, then I wash my hands in the sink using Mom's favorite liquid soap. It smells like summer. When I look in the mirror, I notice that I have dark circles under my eyes. I guess I didn't sleep that well last night. Hiding under Steve's bed was stressful. No wonder I couldn't really get back to sleep. I keep thinking about what would have happened if he'd caught me under his bed. It's really stressing me out even though it didn't happen.

I do that sometimes. When I do something really scary, like hiding from Steve under his bed, I go through a list of possibilities in my head. I wonder what might've happened if he'd caught me. Would he have killed me? Would he have added my head to his collection? Or would he have just slapped me around and turned me over to Mom and Dad? That might be worse than death. At least they couldn't scream at me or ground me if I was nothing more than a head in a bowling ball bag. But that's the kind of stuff my mind does. Sometimes I wonder if me and my mind are working against each other. All I want is to have fun. All it wants to do is stress out.

"You look tired," someone says. It's Steve. He's standing in the doorway. I try not to act scared. He might suspect something.

I quickly think of a lie. "The storm kept me up."

"Me, too," he says. I know he's lying but I don't say anything.

"Why aren't you at work?" I ask.

"I'm getting ready to leave," he says as he checks his hair in the mirror. "What time do you think it is, anyway?"

"I don't know," I tell him. "My clock is blinking."

"It's not even nine yet," he tells me. "Got the whole day ahead of you."

"Yeah," I say.

"What're you gonna do today?" he asks.

"Watch movies," I tell him. "Mom took me to the video store."

"Get anything good?" He's still checking his hair. His cowlick won't stay down. He licks the palm of his hand and tries again.

"Got *Hellraiser* and *Street Trash*," I tell him.

Steve smiles. "Good choices. *Street Trash* is pretty cool."

Since we're talking about movies, I decide to ask him about his movie collection. I know that Mom won't take me back to the video store when David sleeps over. I know she'll say she's already spent too much money on me this week. Steve has a ton of horror movies that I haven't seen because he doesn't like me going through his stuff. But since I've gotten older, he's let me go through his stuff occasionally. Maybe he'll let to do it today. I've been pretty good with his stuff lately. It's been a long time since I've returned a broken movie or a scratched CD.

"Can I ask you something?" I'm still watching him in the mirror. He's really not paying that much attention to me.

"What?" he asks. He stops fixing his hair and looks at me.

"Can I look through your movie collection? David's spending the night tonight." I can tell by the look on his face that he doesn't like the idea.

"I dunno," he says. "I don't like David."

This is the first I've heard about this. "You don't like David?"

"He's a wimp," he says with a snort. "A geek."

"Am I a geek, too?" My feelings are hurt. David's my best friend. I hate it when people make fun of other people just because of the way they look and act.

"You're my brother," he laughs. "You don't count."

"Thanks," I say. I don't really mean it, though.

"It's nothing against you," he explains. He sighs and shrugs his shoulders. "I don't see why not. Just be careful with my shit, okay?"

"Okay," I say. "I'm always careful with your things."

"Now you are," he says. "You didn't used to be."

"But I'm older now." It's true.

"I know. That's why I'm letting you look through 'em." He looks at the digital watch on his arm. "Shit. I gotta run."

"See you tonight?" I ask.

"Yeah, right," he says with a snort. "Like you give a fuck if I get home at a decent time or not." He chuckles. "I'll leave my bedroom unlocked."

I really don't know what to say this time. Not even "yeah" or "okay" sounds like it would work right now. Instead, I just look in the mirror. I look right into my eyes. Steve runs his fingers through his hair one last time and takes off down the stairs. He doesn't even say goodbye. Sometimes it's cool to have a big brother, especially when he lets me look through his CDs or his movies. But sometimes it really sucks, like when he's mean to Mom and Dad and me. His moods are so random that you never know which Steve you're gonna get. It's important to stay out of his way until you know which one you're dealing with. That's how we stay safe.

Downstairs I hear Steve close the front door. He doesn't even bother to lock it. I guess he doesn't care if someone gets inside the house when I'm home alone. That really doesn't surprise me, though. Steve doesn't care about anyone but himself. Dad says it all the time. He calls him "self-serving," like the pumps at the gas station down the street. All I know is that Steve only does stuff if it benefits him. Why he's nice to me sometimes is a mystery. I'm not going to question it, though.

I go downstairs and lock the front door. I don't want anyone to sneak in the house while I'm upstairs. After that, I go into the kitchen to fix some cereal. Once my cereal is in the bowl and swimming in milk, I grab a spoon from the silverware drawer and make my way back upstairs. A chill runs up my back as I pass Steve's room. I'm still spooked from last night. Going in there to look at his movies might be scary.

I've never heard Steve talk the way he did last night. It sounded like two different people living inside his body. And what was all that laughing about? I know he's a murderer, but I didn't know he was a *crazed* murderer. That makes everything different. Does he laugh like a maniac when he's hacking away at someone? What else does he do to them? If he's as crazy as he seems, there's no telling what else he does to their bodies. It's enough to make me lose my appetite. Before that happens, I quickly think of something else. No sense in ruining my day off with thoughts of Steve and his horrible, bloody hobby. Instead, I pop in *Hellraiser* and eat my cereal.

I have the perfect bedroom for watching movies. I don't have a really good TV, but I've got a really cool place to sit and watch them. Since I have thick blue curtains over the windows, most of the sunlight is blocked out. When I'm watching horror movies, I only keep the lamp next to my bed on. It has a really cool shade that makes everything look warm. On my walls are all sorts of movie posters. On my entertainment center are action figures from some of my favorite movies. It's the perfect room to relax in. I'm glad I've got a cool place to relax.

Hellraiser is a pretty weird movie. It's about a puzzle box that opens a gateway to Hell. If you complete the puzzle, these creatures called Cenobites come and drag you away. But this one guy manages to escape from them. With the help of his ex-girlfriend he begins to grow out of the floor of her attic. She murders strangers and he uses their flesh to regenerate himself. It's pretty gross. I've seen it about a dozen times. If someone asks me what my favorite horror movies are, *Hellraiser* is almost always in the top five. My favorites change every day, though.

I'm halfway through the movie when the telephone rings.

Since I don't have a telephone in my room, I run into my parent's bedroom and check the caller ID. I don't recognize the number. Instead of picking it up, I wait until the answering machine picks up. This is called "screening your calls." My parents almost always screen their phone calls. They don't like to talk to people unless it's really important. They never avoid family or friends, but they always avoid people who are trying to sell them something. Those people usually call when we're sitting down for dinner. Dad calls them bad words.

"You've reached 555-6833," the answer machine echoes from the living room. Dad recorded the message. "Leave your name, number, and a brief message after the tone and we'll try to get back with you as soon as possible." Beep.

"It's Steve." He must be calling on his cell phone. "Pick up, Marty." I take a few steps away from the phone. What does he want? "Pick up," he says. I don't pick up the phone. I don't want to hear what he has to say.

"Hang up," I say to myself. "Please."

"Fine," he snaps. "I've changed my mind. Stay outta my room today. I'll let you in tonight. It's a mess and I don't want you making things worse."

Then he hangs up. The answering machine beeps again.

Since Steve's moods come and go without warning, this really doesn't surprise me. He's always saying one thing and doing another. Why doesn't he want me in his room? Did he add another head to his collection? Did he leave it sitting on his bed? Was he too tired from murdering last night to clean up his mess? I'm scared and curious. A big part of me wants to see what he's hiding. But I'm scared to death of what I might find. Just because I look at his severed heads doesn't mean I'm used to them. They still give me the creeps. To me it's just like watching a horror movie.

I go into the hallway and stand in front of his bedroom door.

"After *Hellraiser*," I say to myself. I guess I'm crazy, too. "Then you can look around all you want."

But I'm not listening to myself right now.

I open Steve's bedroom door and slowly creep inside.

Steve's bedroom is a mess. He never picked up after his little fit last night. Clothes and papers and all sorts of stuff cover his floor. My eyes immediately go towards the closet doors. I fight the urge to open them up and take a look inside the bag. If he did kill again last night, his trophy would be in there. But I'm too nervous and scared to take a look. I don't think I could handle something like that right now. I might start crying. I might throw up my cereal. Hearing Steve talk like a psychopath was just too creepy. Imagining my brother murdering a helpless, defenseless black woman isn't something I need to think about right now. It's just too much.

Instead, I head directly to his movie collection.

Steve's been collecting movies since he was a teenager. He's got tons of them. Not all of them are horror movies, though. He's got some comedies, a few action movies, and one or two dramas. But all of them are dark in one way or another. None of the comedies are ones my parents would like. The action movies are from Japan and contain lots and lots of violence. And the dramas talk about things that make most people uncomfortable. He's got one of the coolest collections. It's even better than the video store. I'm glad I'm getting old enough for Steve to trust me with his stuff. Sometimes I wish Steve were just a normal big brother. Then we could eat popcorn and watch these movies together. We would talk about our favorite parts and quote our favorite lines.

Most of his movies are on VHS, though he does have a few on DVD. I can't watch the ones on DVD because I don't have a player in my bedroom. Even if I did, Steve's DVDs come from overseas and require a special kind of player. So I just ignore those since I want to spend the day in my bedroom. Besides, I don't think Steve would like it if I spent the day watching DVDs in his bedroom. That might cross the line. And I don't want to piss Steve off. He might decide not to let me look at his movie collection anymore. That would definitely suck. I wouldn't like that.

There's a few movies that I'd love to watch. One of them is called *Paperhouse*. It's about a little girl who draws a house while she's sick and visits it in her dreams. There's another one called *The Ring*, which is about a video tape that kills you seven days after you watch it. I've seen that one before but it's one of my favorites. He's also got another one called *Nightbreed*, which is by the guy who directed *Hellraiser*. His name is Clive Barker. Steve reads his books but I really don't like to read that much. I spend too much time reading in school.

All of Steve's movies have the original boxes. And all of them are in really good condition. That's why the one with the cracked, clear box really makes me stop and think for a second. Most places don't sell movies without the original box. And this clear box reminds me of the kind they have in video stores. I pull it out of its space. I'm careful not to knock any of the others over. I turn it the right way so I can read the title. This makes me smile. I should have known Steve had this.

In my hands is the video store's stolen copy of *Headless*.

But why would Steve steal a movie from a video store? That's a stupid question, I guess. Why does Steve do any of things he does? The only reason I can think of is that he couldn't find it anywhere else. That means he couldn't order it off the Internet or find it at that little store downtown that sells rare and hard-to-find movies and CDs. Steve must really like this movie to actually steal it from a video store. How do you steal a movie from a video store, anyway? They have that alarm system that goes off anytime you walk through it with a movie. He must be good at stealing, too.

Inside the box for *Headless* is folded piece of notebook paper. I sit down on Steve's bed and open the case. The notebook paper feels old and the creases look like they're about to tear. I carefully unfold it and turn it right-side up. Written on the paper in sloppy handwriting are times and descriptions. For example, a woman's head is sliced off while she's having sex nine minutes into the film. And another woman's head is removed while she's sleeping fifteen minutes later. It also says that this woman has her eyes removed with a spoon. My hands start to shake. I let the paper slide from my fingers. It slowly falls to the floor. I think I've found something important.

I've think I've found where Steve gets his ideas from.

I don't know which happened first, though. Did Steve see the movie and then start killing or did he start killing and then use *Headless* as a guideline? The idea that Steve uses this movie as inspiration makes me feel dirty. But I still want to see the movie, though. But it's not a horror movies anymore. It's a way to help me understand what Steve does and how he does it. He's even made himself a little map of the movie. If he needs a new idea for a murder, I guess he just fast forwards the tape to one of the times on the paper and gets inspired. I count the number of descriptions on the page. I guess there's at least twenty-nine murders in this movie. That's a lot of murders for a horror movie. It must not have much of a story.

But I guess he's not watching it for the story.

I always thought Steve was working with his own imagination. I thought that all those heads were severed using ideas he came up with on his own. I guess he's not that original. Will horror movies make me want to kill people, too? I think I'm a littler smarter than that. Besides, I'm not a violent person. I don't even like killing bugs. I can't even defend myself against bullies in the school bathroom. How would I ever have the courage to take out a knife and put an end to someone's life?

Headless is no longer a horror movie. It's a way to understand Steve. It's a way to get to know my big brother. I'll take anything I can get. I used to love having Steve as a big brother. But now that he's older and meaner and a killer, I don't feel as close to him as I used to. I don't think we'll ever be as close as we used to be. Our family's just different now. We all act differently towards each other.

I fold the paper and stick it back inside the clear case. Once it's closed I tuck it under my arm. I don't feel comfortable watching *Headless* by myself. I don't think I could handle it. I'd think of Steve the entire time. I'd picture him holding an axe or a meat cleaver or a knife, standing above a screaming, crying, helpless black woman. I'd picture him grabbing her by the hair and slicing her head off. I'd picture him holding the head up high and laughing that crazy laugh he did last night. That's not something I want to think about when I'm home alone.

I decide to save this one for when David spends the night. That way I won't be by myself when the blood starts to flow.

The rest of the morning and afternoon is spent watching *Hellraiser* and *Street Trash*. Even though both movies have enough gore and violence to keep me happy, I can't stop thinking about Steve and his movie. Every once in a while I'll look over at the clear case. I think about what it contains. I think about which scenes Steve's used and which scenes he hasn't. I think about how Steve might react if he finds out I borrowed one of his movies after he told me to stay out of his room. I could just tell him I'd already picked it out before he called. This way he won't be able to yell at me. I just hope he doesn't mind me borrowing *Headless* since it means so much to him.

It's been a tiring morning.

Once *Street Trash* is over, I fall asleep.

CHAPTER 9

▼

DAVID

"Marty?" It's a familiar voice.

I open my eyes a little and see Mom standing over my bed. She looks worried. I smile and roll over onto my back.

"Hey," I say.

"Are you feeling okay?" she asks.

"I'm all right," I tell her. "Why?"

"Because you're asleep," she says. I can tell she's still worried. I can hear it in her voice. "David will be here in about an hour."

I totally forgot about David spending the night. Usually I spend a few hours getting ready for him to show up. I'll get some games together, get some movies together, and make sure we have enough food and drinks to get us through the night. If you don't have enough to eat or drink then it really takes away from how much fun you can have. I can't believe I slept the afternoon away. I feel like I've wasted my free time. It's not everyday that I get a free day off from school. I'm pretty upset with myself that I spent most of the day asleep on my bed.

"I'll get up," I tell her. I put my feet on the floor. "Can we order a pizza?"

"What about your stomach?" she asks.

Pizza gives me gas. Really bad gas. Gas that stinks up the bathroom when I sit down on the toilet. It comes out quietly which means that it's going to stink pretty bad. Mom always says she's not going to order pizza for me again, but she always ends up doing it anyway. It's my own fault for eating the pizza, but I can't help it. It's one of my favorite foods. I'd eat it all the time if I could.

"I'll be okay," I tell her.

"Yeah, right," she says. The look on her face says that she doesn't believe me. "You say that every time. Then you spend a few hours in the bathroom."

She's right. "I'll be okay," I say again. "I really want some pizza."

"Okay," she says. "But it's your funeral."

I don't know what to say.

"Did you enjoy your day off?" she asks.

"Yeah," I tell her. "It was fun. I watched those movies I rented."

"Were they good?"

"They were pretty good. I've seen *Hellraiser* before." Mom can't keep track of what movies I've seen. That's because movies aren't Mom's favorite thing in the whole world. Mom's favorite thing in the whole world is reading. She says that the pictures in her head are much better than the pictures on a television. Sometimes she's right. There are a few books I've read that didn't turn out to be very good movies.

As Mom is about to leave the room she stops in the doorway and says, "Are you sure you want a pizza? Can I fix you something else?"

"No," I tell her. "I want a pepperoni pizza. Is that okay?"

"Like I said," she tells me. "Your funeral."

Mom goes downstairs to fix dinner for her and Dad and Steve. Even though Steve rarely eats with us she still makes enough for him anyway. He always stops on the way home from work and eats fast food. At least that's what he says he does. I can't imagine eating fast food everyday. Our health teacher at school says that eating fast food everyday will make you fat, tired, and will cause health problems in the future. I like fast food, but I don't want to be sick when I get older. I want to enjoy being older. What's the point of getting older if you can't enjoy it?

After she goes downstairs, I start getting things together in my room. When David spends the night, we usually spend most of the time in my bedroom. We play video games, listen to music, watch movies, talk about people at school, draw comics, and try our best to have fun. Tonight we'll probably work on one of our comic books, watch *Headless*, and spend the rest of the night listening to music. We might talk about some people from school, too. I want to make sure that David has fun when he spends the night. If he doesn't, I might lose him as a friend.

And I don't have many friends.

It takes me a while to get everything ready. I put away my dirty clothes, put away some of the junk on my desk and bed, and make sure that everything we need is already in my room. The only thing I don't have in here already is something to drink. I decide to leave that in the refrigerator. That way it can stay cold. Going downstairs for something to drink in the middle of the night can be a little scary if you've just finished a really good horror movie. But that's part of the fun. David likes to try to scare me. He's the one who gets freaked out most of the time, though.

Around the time I'm done, the doorbell rings.

"Marty!" Mom calls from the kitchen. "David's here!"

I run downstairs and answer the door.

David's standing on the porch. He's got his backpack on one shoulder. Even though he's smiling he doesn't look that happy to be here. David's a little taller than I am with messy brown hair and really bright blue eyes. They're really bright because he wears contacts. Lots of people think David is very handsome. Mom is one of those people. She says it's because he has really attractive parents. His parents look like they could be in a fashion magazine. They have really good skin and really good teeth and their smiles are perfect. Dad doesn't like his parents. He thinks they're snotty.

"Hey," I say.

"Hey," he says.

I step out of the way so that he can come in. I close the front door and lock it back. "My parents said that I have to leave by noon tomorrow," he says. "I gotta go outta town. My cousin's getting married in Danville tomorrow."

"That sucks," I say. "My Dad's taking me to a movie tomorrow."

"Really?" He doesn't sound that excited about it.

"Yeah," I tell him. "A horror movie."

"That's cool," he says.

"Mom!" I shout. "David's here!"

She comes into the living room from the kitchen. "Hey, David," she says with a big smile. "How are you tonight?"

"Pretty good," he says. "My mom told me to tell you hi."

"That's sweet," she says. I wonder if she really means it.

"Can you order the pizza?" I ask.

Mom gives me a look. "Are you sure about that?"

David laughs. "He gets gas," he says.

"That he does," Mom says with a sigh. "I'll order your pizza for you."

"Thanks," I say.

She doesn't say anything as she goes back into the kitchen. David and I go upstairs to my bedroom. He takes off his backpack and tosses it onto the bed. "I brought some stuff," he tells me as he unzips it. "Is that okay?"

"Like what?" I ask.

He pulls out two VHS tapes. "I brought *Dead Alive* and *Bad Taste*. My sister's boyfriend let me borrow them. He says they're classic."

I've seen both of those movies before but I don't tell David that. He seems pretty excited about bringing them and I don't want to ruin his fun. David doesn't bring movies over that often. Even though his parents are rich and they pretty much give him anything he wants, he doesn't have a very big movie collection. He's more into video games. I think the only reason he likes horror movies is because I like horror movies. It gives us something to do. It's something we have in common.

"Cool," I tell him. "I've got a movie for us to watch, too."

"What?" he asks. He sits down on the edge of my bed.

"It's called *Headless*," I tell him. I point to the clear case on my entertainment center. "My brother stole it from the video store."

"He stole it?" He starts to laugh a little.

"Yeah," I say. It is kinda funny. "I don't know when he stole it, but he stole it."

"Is it gross?" David asks.

"I dunno," I tell him. "I haven't seen it yet."

"Cool," he says. "Which one do you wanna watch first?"

"Let's watch *Bad Taste*," I say. "We'll watch *Headless* after it gets dark."

"Wanna work on our graphic novel while we watch it?" He starts taking some pencils and paper from his backpack. "I came up with a new character during math today. He's pretty cool. His name is Carnival Sin."

He mentioned school. I don't want to talk about school.

But I need to know what happened.

"Did anyone say anything about me today?" I ask. I'm really nervous. "About what happened in the bathroom yesterday?"

David stops unpacking his backpack. "Yeah." That's all he says.

"Like what?" I really don't want to know.

He takes a deep breath. "Are you sure you wanna know?"

"I guess," I say. I'm really not sure.

"Well, Leroy told everyone you had a really small dick and that you tried to kiss them," he says. "Marcus wasn't there today, though. He skips school all the time." David gives me a look. "I guess that's why you weren't at school today, huh?"

"Yeah," I say. I can't stop thinking about yesterday. Every time I try to think about something else my thoughts get jumbled.

I figured they'd tell everyone that I had a small penis. That really doesn't surprise me. And he told me yesterday that they told everyone I tried to kiss them. That's just a bold-faced lie, though. What I'm really worried about are the nicknames. I don't want people to make up nicknames for me just because Leroy said I had a small penis. I can handle him telling people lies because I know they're not true. It's when those lies turn into mean names that I start to get really upset. Being made fun of is my worst fear. I pray to God every night that people leave me alone at school. God doesn't listen to me, though. He just lets them do whatever they want to.

"They didn't even get a look at it," I tell David.

"I know," he says. "I talked to Randy at recess. He told me what happened."

I'll have to thank Randy on Monday.

"Does everyone know?" I ask.

David just looks at me. "What's it matter?"

"It just does," I say. "I want to know if I have to worry or not."

"Leroy and Marcus are always picking on someone," he says. "It was just your turn. On Monday it will be someone else. Don't worry about it."

I don't know how not to worry about it. All I do is worry. I worry about homework. I worry about tests. I worry about my family. I worry about Steve's victims. I worry that I'll come home one day and there will be blood everywhere. I worry that Steve will murder Mom and Dad because he hates them so much. I worry that he might even murder me. All I do is worry. I don't know how to make it stop.

"I guess," I finally say. I take a deep breath and try to relax. I tell myself that relaxation is very important. "I just wanted to know."

"Well, stop talking about it," he says. "Let's watch *Bad Taste* and work on our graphic novel. I'm done talking about school."

We work on the comic and watch the movie until the pizza arrives. Mom brings it upstairs and hands it to me. I set it on the bed and open the box. The smell fills the room. I love the smell of pepperoni pizza. It's one of my favorite smells in the world. We stop working on the comic because we don't want to get grease all over the pictures. We spend the rest of the movie eating pizza and laughing at all the violence. It's a really funny movie. By the time the movie is over, all of the pizza is gone. I can feel my belly starting to get upset. The gas is starting to set in.

And then I fart.

"Jesus," David laughs. "You got gas already?"

I'm really uncomfortable. I make an uncomfortable face. "I don't feel good."

"You're stupid," he says. Then he shakes his head.

"But it's good," I tell him. "I'd eat another one right now."

David sniffs the air. "Goddamn," he says. David uses bad words all the time. "That's pretty nasty, man. Do that in the bathroom."

I fart again. "I'm sorry."

He points to the door. "Go."

I run to the bathroom, shut the door, and squat down on the floor. I don't like taking a dump. I don't like wiping my butt. Most of the time I just smear the mess all over my butt and spend ten minutes trying to clean myself up. When I don't want to take a dump, I kneel down on one knee and squeeze my butt cheeks together. As I squeeze them together, little baby farts make their way out of my butt. The bathroom starts to smell bad. I stand up and turn on the fan. David was right. It is pretty nasty. I'm starting to wonder if I should've eaten that pizza. My stomach is so swollen.

While I'm farting in the bathroom, I hear someone stomping up the stairs. It's gotta be Steve. He's the only one who walks up the stairs like that. I hear him open his bedroom door and slam it shut. He must be in one of his moods. I probably shouldn't tell him that I already picked out a movie. You don't talk to Steve about anything when he's upset. There's no point. Whatever you say or whatever you do is going to be wrong. It just is. We all know to stay out of his way when he's upset.

I wipe my butt just to make sure I didn't squirt anything out when I was farting. After I'm cleaned up and the bathroom light is turned off, I go back to my bedroom. David's still sitting on the bed. He's looking through the comic we've been working on. I pick up the clear case on my entertainment center and pop it open. The folded piece of paper inside falls onto the floor and I kick it under the bed. I don't want David to see it. I don't want him to know about Steve's list.

"Wanna watch *Headless*?" I ask.

"Sure," he says. He doesn't look up from the comic. "Is it good?"

"I haven't seen it," I tell him. "I told you that."

He doesn't say anything. He's too busy reading the comic book.

I eject the other movie and slide *Headless* into the VCR. Once I make sure it's playing and everything's okay, I crawl onto the bed and sit beside David. "Put down the book," I tell him. "This is supposed to be pretty cool."

"Violent?" he asks.

"Of course." Horror movies aren't horror movies unless they're violent.

The FBI warning comes on the screen. It tells us not to play the movie in public or make any illegal copies or we'll go to jail. How do they know if I make a copy or not? Do they send FBI agents to people's homes to look through their movie collections for anything that's not legal? I think the FBI warnings are like your parents telling you not to do something. As long as you get away with it and it doesn't hurt anyone, then there's really not a problem. At least that's what I think.

"Do you need anything to drink?" I ask.

"I'm good," he says. Then he yawns. "Gettin' tired, though."

That's not a good sign. "Seriously?"

"I went to school today, remember?" he says. "You didn't."

He has a very good point. Usually I'm pretty tired by the end of the day. School takes a lot out of you. You spend all day thinking and reading and adding and subtracting. Multiplying and dividing. Worrying and wondering. My parents are always complaining about being tired when they get home from work. When I mention that I'm tired, too, they look at me like I'm a freak. Don't they understand that school is hard work? Is that such a weird thing to say? They went to school, too. Maybe they don't remember how hard it was. Maybe school wasn't that hard when they were young.

I try to stop thinking so much so I can't watch the movie in peace.

There aren't any previews to sit through. No credits, either.

The title appears on the TV in big red letters that drip like blood.

And then the movie begins.

CHAPTER 10

▼

HEADLESS

Headless is really scary.

But not scary like some horror movies are. There aren't any ghosts that jump out and try to scare you. The music doesn't get really loud when something spooky happens. It's scary because every time the killer cuts someone's head off, I just imagine Steve doing that to some poor black woman. It's scary because I can picture Steve doing horrible things to people just like the killer does in the movie. I think about getting the piece of paper from under my bed that has all the times written on it. I want to see which murders Steve had written down but I don't want David to see it. There'd be too much to explain if he did see it. He doesn't need to know about Steve.

The first killing happens as soon as the movie starts. The killer has a naked black woman tied up in mid-air. Her arms are tied to the ceiling and her feet are tied to the floor. She's hanging in the middle of this empty room that has drains in the floor. I'm not sure where it's supposed to take place because they never show you if the room is in the killer's house or not. All it shows is the woman, the ropes, and the drains. She has a piece of silver tape across her mouth so she can't make any noise. When they show a close-up of her eyes, she looks very scared.

Then the killer enters the room.

He wears a weird mask shaped like a skull that looks like it was made in art class using construction paper. It has blood all over it. In his hand is a very long, very sharp machete that looks like the one Dad uses to cut dead limbs off the tree in our backyard. It also has blood all over it. The woman starts to move around when she sees the killer. She tries to scream but the tape over her mouth stops it from getting too loud. She starts to cry. They show a close-up of her eyes again and the tears just keep falling. It looks and feels very real. I almost turn off the tape because it feels so real.

"This is stupid," David says. "Isn't it?"

"I don't know," I say. "I haven't seen it yet."

"Why is she tied up?" he asks.

"I don't know," I say again. David is getting on my nerves. I just want to see the movie because it might help explain why Steve does the things he does. I'm not watching the movie because it's good. I'm watching it because it's educational.

The killer walks up to the woman and begins to rub the machete across her naked body. He rubs it against her breasts and then he rubs it between her legs. Her eyes are wide and scared. The killer smacks the woman across the face with the back of his hand every time she starts to move around. Then he turns around like he's done playing with her. And just when you think he's going to leave her alone, he turns around really quick and swings the machete. Both of her breasts are cut right off her body. Blood splatters all over the place. The woman screams and screams through the tape.

"Gross!" David says. He's smiling and laughing. "That's great!"

"Yeah," I say. I feel sick. "Great."

"That's the sickest shit I've ever seen," he tells me. I think so, too.

The killer swings the machete again. This time it cuts off her left leg right below the knee. Blood spurts from the stump. The woman screams louder. Then he does the same thing to the other leg. Pools and pools of blood cover the floor. There's a close-up of a drain as blood flows down it. The woman is hanging in the air by her arms since both of her legs have been cut off below the knees. When they show a close-up of both bloody stumps, you can see a tube pumping fake blood onto the floor.

"Look!" David laughs. He points at the TV. "You can see the tube they pump the fake blood through! That's so stupid!"

It doesn't matter to me. It all seems too real.

Someone knocks on my bedroom door. I pause the movie with the remote control.

Mom opens the door and sticks her head in. "You boys okay?"

"Yeah," I tell her.

"We're okay," David says. He closes his eyes and smiles stupidly.

Mom laughs. "We're going to bed," she tells us. "Keep it down to a dull roar, okay? I've gotta work tomorrow."

"Okay," I tell her.

"Goodnight," David says. He likes my mom because he thinks she's pretty.

"Goodnight, boys," she tells us. Then she shuts the door.

I look at the clock. It's close to midnight.

"This movie is stupid," David says. "And your brother is sick."

I don't know what to say. He's right, though.

I start the movie again and the killer is leaning in close to the woman's face. Her eyes are rolling back in her skull. He takes a few steps back, screams like he's going crazy, and swings the machete at her face. The blade cuts right through her neck. As blood explodes from her neck, her head falls from her body and rolls across the floor. Her whole body starts to shake. Blood is all over the place. I've never seen a horror movie show so much blood in the first ten minutes. I've seen gore movies before but this one is really, really gross. I don't think I like it.

The killer picks up the severed head with his free hand and looks into the eyes. She's dead. He laughs as he looks at the head. It reminds me of the laughter I heard that night when I was hiding under Steve's bed. It's the same kind of crazy laugh. Only crazed serial killers laugh like that. I wonder if Steve learned to laugh that way by watching this movie or if all killers laugh like that after they've cut the head off a beautiful woman. I bet he learned it from this movie.

After he's done laughing at the severed head, the movie cuts to the outside of an abandoned building. The killer opens the front door and walks outside to his car. He's still got the head in one hand and the bloody machete in the other. He gets in his car, puts the head in the passenger seat, and drives away. When he gets home to his apartment building, he climbs the fire escape and enters his apartment through the window. That reminds me of Steve. He climbs through windows, too. After he's inside and the window is shut and locked, the killer takes off his mask.

His face is covered with long scars and ugly burns.

"That's pretty cool," David says.

"Why are the killers always so ugly?" I ask.

"Huh?" David looks at me funny.

"I bet there are some killers that look like you and me," I explain. "I bet not all killers look like that. Some of them are probably normal."

"How do you know?" David asks.

"I'm just guessing," I tell him. I don't want to tell him about Steve.

The killer sits down at the desk in his bedroom and takes out a small scalpel from one of the drawers. Then he carefully cuts out both eyes from the severed head and pops both of them in his mouth. As he starts to chew, nasty stuff starts to ooze out of his mouth. It looks like melted butter. The killer doesn't seem to mind the taste. He just chews and swallows the eyeballs like he was eating regular food. I guess this isn't the first time he's eaten someone's eyes. My stomach starts to hurt a little bit. I can't stop imagining Steve doing the exact same thing.

Maybe that's why he's not hungry when he gets home from work. Maybe he lies about getting fast food. Maybe he likes the taste of eyeballs. I start to think about other details from the movie. Like the mask and the machete. Does Steve use a machete to kill his victims? Does he wear a weird mask when he's doing it so they can't see his face? And does he cut off other parts of their body before finally cutting off their heads? It's almost too much to think about. I look over at David. He's smiling. He doesn't know how real this stuff is. He doesn't know that there's a real head collector sleeping in the bedroom next door. He just doesn't know.

After the killer has cut out the eyes, he takes off his pants and his underwear. They actually show his penis. It's sticking straight out like a faucet. He takes the head off the desk and puts his penis inside one of the eye sockets and starts having sex with it. In and out. Back and forth. David looks and me and I look at him. He makes a face like he might be sick. I might be sick, too.

"Fucking gross!" he laughs. "This is the sickest movie I've ever seen."

I can't think straight. All I see is Steve.

"You okay?" David asks.

I feel really sick. "This movie is gross," I say.

"Are you sick?" he asks. Then he laughs. "You big pussy."

"I'm not sick because of the movie," I lie. "It's because of the pizza."

"Yeah, right," he says. He laughs again. "This movie is too much for you. Too adult. Maybe you should stick to PG-13 horror movies."

"Shut-up," I tell him. I hate being teased.

"What's this thing rated?" he asks.

"I don't know," I tell him. "I think it's unrated."

"That makes sense," he says.

After the he's done having sex with the head and there's white stuff oozing from the eye socket, the killer opens up his bedroom closet and takes out a black bowling ball bag. He unzips the bag, takes out the bowling ball, and puts the head inside the bag. He zips it up, puts it back in his closet, and closes the door.

Then the screen goes black.

Everything in this movie has inspired Steve. Everything from the severing of heads to hiding them in bowling ball bags. I wonder if Steve has sex with the heads like the killer does. I wonder if Steve does everything he sees in the movie. I can't get the mental images of Steve doing all these things out of my head. My stomach starts to hurt really bad. I feel like I need to go to the bathroom. I feel like I might mess my pants. Messing my pants in front of David isn't a good idea.

I pause the movie. "I'll be right back."

"Gonna be sick, pussy?" David laughs really hard. It's not that funny.

"Shut-up," I tell him. I try to sound mean but all it does it make David laugh harder. I hate it when he laughs at me.

I leave the bedroom and shut the door. Out in the hallway I can hear Dad and Steve talking downstairs. It sounds like they're arguing about something. That's nothing new. They never talk about the weather or sports or movies or anything. They always argue about stuff. I stand near the bathroom door and listen. Dad calls Steve spoiled. Steve calls Dad a fucking hypocrite. I hear the front door open and then I hear it slam shut. Then Dad starts walking up the stairs.

I run in the bathroom and shut the door before he get upstairs.

I lean against the back of the door and listen carefully. Dad mumbles as he goes into his bedroom. Steve must've left again. I feel a little better. Having Steve sleeping next door tonight wouldn't make me feel very safe. The movie has really gotten under my skin. The movie is making me even more afraid of Steve. I'm glad that he's gone out for the night. Even though the rest of Lexington's not safe, it's nice to know that I am. That makes me sound selfish. Maybe I am.

I go back to my bedroom after I'm done using the bathroom.

"Did you shit yourself?" David says.

"I'm getting tired of you picking on me," I tell him. I'm very serious. The last thing I need is to have my best friend treat me like everyone else at school does.

"I'm just playing," he tells me. "Chill out."

I can't chill out. And I'm not a pussy. And I didn't mess myself. I'm braver than most people think. I sneak into Steve's room when I'm not supposed to. I open Steve's closet and look at his severed heads. I'm a brave person. Most people wouldn't do some of the stuff that I do. I don't think a person who isn't brave could look at a severed head and keep from screaming. I don't think a person who isn't brave could handle that kind of horror. David couldn't handle the stuff that I've seen. David couldn't handle seeing a real severed head. He'd be the one to mess his pants.

"Sit down," David says. "I won't pick on you."

I sit down and start the movie again.

The rest of it is just as nasty.

There really isn't a story to follow. The killer goes to work at a factory during the day and murders black women at night. He attacks one black woman as she's leaving work. He cuts her into pieces using that machete and throws everything into a nearby dumpster. Everything except the head. He has sex with it in the mouth and then throws the head off a bridge. The next victim is a black prostitute he picks up downtown. He takes her back to his apartment and does horrible things to her. Horrible things. I can't even talk about the things he does to her. There's more killings and more killings and more killings. I've never seen so many deaths in a horror movie before.

And all of the victims are black women.

"This movie is racist," David says about half-way through the movie. "Is your brother racist or something?"

"I don't think so," I lie. Steve's pretty racist. He uses the "N" word more often than I think anyone is really supposed to. Mom hates it when he says that word. She's asked him not to use it around her, but he does anyway. That's why it doesn't surprise me that he uses this movie as a study guide for his own killing spree.

We watch the rest of the movie without saying anything to each other. I think David is bored. Sometimes he looks around the room like he's looking for something better to do. I can't stop watching the movie. I'm so scared that my hands won't stop shaking. All I can think about is Steve. Whenever the killer is doing something nasty to someone, I see Steve in his place. I see Steve's smiling face as he cuts off the heads. I see Steve's smiling face when he's having sex with the severed heads. I see Steve's smiling face when he puts the heads in the black bowling ball bag.

David looks at my hands. "Are you shaking?"

"No," I say.

"Yes you are," David says. He's smiling. "You're scared."

"No I'm not." Why is he picking on me?

"You're fucking scared of a movie," he laughs. "Is this too much for you?"

"I'm not scared," I tell him. "I'm not kidding."

"You're not kidding?" He points at my hands. "You're shaking."

I hide my hands under my legs. "Stop looking at my hands, David. Geez."

He won't stop laughing. "Little Marty's afraid of a movie."

I don't understand why he's picking on me. Usually I don't act this way during horror movies but it's different this time. He just doesn't understand how real this is. There's probably a severed head in Steve's bedroom closet right now. If

David knew this he wouldn't make fun of me for being afraid. He wouldn't sit there and laugh at me like he is right now. I think about showing him Steve's bowling ball bag just to make him leave me alone. That would probably shut him up.

The movie ends with the cops busting down the killer's door while he's trying to murder his landlord. She's naked on the floor and he's on top of her with that machete in his hand. Right before he cuts off her head, the police bust in and shoot him at least ten times in the back. The landlord screams and screams as blood splatters all over her face and in her mouth. As they shoot him the killer throws the machete at the cops. He misses and hits the wall instead. Then he falls on top of his landlord and dies. The screen fades to black and the movie ends.

I stop the tape and start rewinding it.

"That was weak," David says. "Really fucking weak."

"Be quiet," I tell him. I put my finger up to my mouth. "Don't cuss so loud."

"But it was weak," he says. "Fake and weak."

"It was sick," I tell him. I shake my head. "Too sick."

"Are you kidding?" He gets off the bed and stretches. "That was the weakest horror movie I've ever seen. It didn't even have a story."

"It's a slasher movie," I explain. "They don't have good stories."

"Well, I don't care what it was. It was weak." David yawns and stretches some more. "Why in the hell did we watch it?"

"I thought it might be good," I say.

"You thought wrong," he says.

I narrow my eyes and glare at him. "What's wrong with you?"

"I'm bored," he says. "I thought we were gonna have some fun tonight."

"I thought we were." I feel sad. I try to make sure that David has fun. I guess I'm not good at it. "What do you want to do now? Watch another movie?"

"I don't think you can handle another one," David says. He laughs at me again.

"I told you I wasn't scared," I tell him.

"Yeah, right." He looks at one of the posters on my wall. "You're lying."

"I am not." I'm getting angry. Why is he acting like this?

"Yeah, you are. You couldn't stop shaking during the whole thing." He turns around. He's got a weird smile on his face.

"What?" I ask.

He chuckles. "Maybe you do have a small penis."

I can't believe my ears. "What did you say?"

"I said maybe you do have a small penis," he says. "Maybe Leroy was right."

I try to fight back the tears but it's really hard to do. I never thought my best friend would say something like that. Sometimes David plays around and jokes with me, but this is just too mean to be a joke. It hurts too much. And he's not smiling now. He's just looking at me. I just don't understand why he's acting like he doesn't want to be my friend anymore. Usually we have lots of fun watching horror movies, even if they are really bad and really fake. They used to be fun.

An idea pops in my head. A really bad idea. But I need to prove to David that I'm not scared of a movie. I need to show him that *Headless* isn't a joke. If he sees one of the severed heads for himself then maybe he'll understand why I was shaking. Maybe he'll understand why this movie got to me. If he understands why, then he might leave me alone. He might stop picking on me.

"You wanna see something really scary?" I ask him.

"Like what?" he says. He doesn't seem that interested in what I have to say.

"Something really scary," I say.

"You mean like the movie we just watched?" I don't like to use bad words but he's really acting like an giant asshole tonight.

"Something scarier," I tell him.

"Go ahead," he says with a smile. "Try to scare me."

I take a deep breath. "Okay," I say. "Let's go."

"Where?" he asks.

"Steve's room," I say. "There's something in there I want to show you."

CHAPTER 11

▼

REVEALED

We step out into the dark hallway.

"Are you sure this is okay?" David asks.

"Are you scared?" I ask.

David smiles. "Scared? Yeah, right."

I tell David to wait upstairs while I run down to the kitchen to get a butter knife. When I get back he's sitting on the floor in front of Steve's bedroom. Even though he says he's not scared I can see in his eyes that's he's not quite sure about what we're going to do. I pop the lock and open the door. David gives me a look and stands up. We slowly enter the darkness of Steve's room. I flip the switch next the door. The overhead light comes on. David looks around and sits down on the edge of Steve's bed. I just hope Steve doesn't come home soon.

"His room's pretty cool," he says.

"I know," I tell him. "He's got a lot of cool horror movies."

"As cool as the one we just watched?" David laughs. He's messing with me again. "I mean, you can't get much cooler than *Headless*."

I don't say anything.

"Are you ignoring me?" David asks.

I turn and look at him. "What's your problem?"

"What?" He acts like he doesn't know what I'm talking about.

"You know what I mean," I tell him. I'm getting very angry. "You've been picking on me all night. Did I do something to you?"

"No," he says. He looks away.

"Are you sure?" I keep looking at him. It's making him nervous.

He takes a breath and looks at me. "Don't you get tired of watching horror movies all the time? Don't you get tired of doing the same thing every time I spend the night? I mean, I like coming over, but we do the exact same thing every time."

This is new to me. "What would *you* like to do?"

"I dunno," he says. "Something different. Something fun. Something that doesn't have anything to do with horror movies."

David's the only person I know that enjoys horror movies. Now he says he doesn't like watching horror movies all the time. When did this happen? That's what we had in common. That's the thing that made us friends in the first place. That and the comic book. I don't understand at all. I'm confused. Does he not like hanging out with me anymore? Would he rather hang out with his other friends from school? I guess they're cooler than I am. David probably has more fun with them.

"Do you wanna see something scary?" I ask.

David just shakes his head. "Whatever, Marty. Do your worst."

I open the closet door and take out the bowling ball bag. It's heavy. It must have a head inside. I put the bag on the bed next to David. He looks at it and smiles. "A bowling ball bag? Are you kidding me? That's supposed to be scary?"

"It's not the bag," I tell him. "It's what Steve's got inside."

"Like the movie, right? I guess there's a head in there." David shakes his head again. I guess he thinks I'm messing around.

"Maybe," I say. "Maybe not."

"You want me to open it?" he asks.

"If you want to," I say. "I'm not going to make you do anything."

David pushes me out of the way and grabs the bag. "Get outta my way."

He sets the bag on the bed and slowly unzips it.

"Are you sure you want to do this?" I ask.

"Shut-up," he says. "This is the last time I spend the night with you."

I watch as he finishes unzipping the bag. There's a funky smell coming from inside. David takes a step back and covers his mouth and nose with his hand. He looks at me. His eyes are wide and he looks like he might cry. Did he see what was inside already? Did he get a look at one of Steve's trophies? I can't tell.

"What did your brother do? Shit in this thing?" he asks.

"What's wrong?" I ask. "Scared?"

"Fuck you," he says. Even though it's a whisper I can tell that he's pretty mad. "You're not gonna fuck with me. Fucking pussy."

"What the hell is wrong with you?" I ask. I've had enough of his attitude. "I don't understand why you're being so mean to me."

"You wanna know what's wrong?" he says. He pushes me again. "It's hard being your friend, Marty. Everyone makes fun of you. And when you're not there, they make fun of me because I'm your friend. You know what that's like?"

"Yeah," I tell him. "I know what that's like."

"It sucks," he says. He pushes me closer to the closet. "I hate taking up for you. I'm sick of it. It makes going to school harder than it should be."

"Then don't do it," I say. "Nobody asked you to stick up for me."

"Good." He gets really close to my face. "I don't wanna be your goddamn friend anymore. You got that?"

I don't believe this. "What? Why?"

"Don't talk to me anymore at school," he says. "I don't want people making fun of me just because I'm friends with you. It's not fair."

I start to cry. I can't help it. "I won't have anybody to talk to."

"Stop crying," he snaps. "Stop it."

I can't stop crying. It just keeps coming.

"I said cut it out." He makes a fist with his right hand. It looks like he might hit with me it. "If you don't stop crying I'll fucking hit you."

"Don't." That's all I can say.

Then he hits me. Right in the jaw. I fall backwards, bounce off the closet doors, and land on my butt. David stands over me with a smile on his face. He looks happy that he punched me. He looks thrilled that he knocked me down. I cry harder. I try not to cry too loud because it might wake up my parents. I don't want them to know that David isn't my friend anymore. I don't want them to know that I'm in Steve's bedroom when I'm not supposed to be. I don't want them to find the severed head in the bowling ball bag. I try to keep quiet but it's really hard.

David picks up the bag. "You want me to open this?"

"I don't care," I say. "Do what you want."

"No," he snaps. I feel like I'm being scolded by my parents. "You wanted me to open this bag so I'm gonna open it. Got it?"

"Whatever," I say. I just don't care anymore.

David turns the bag upside down.

A head falls onto the floor.

Marcus' head.

Marcus Sanders' severed head.

When the head hits the floor, blood pops right out of the neck and onto David's shoes. He takes several steps away from the mess he made. I look into his eyes. He's still trying to figure out what's going on. I bet he thinks it's some sort of joke. He probably thinks I'm trying to make him look like an idiot. Before I can say anything, David starts making weird little gasping sounds. I've never heard anything like it before.

"David?" He doesn't say anything. I stop crying. "David?"

"Is that...?" He stops himself. "Is that Marcus?"

It is Marcus Sanders. Steve must have figured out where he was. I don't know how he did it since Steve doesn't know anything about the kids I go to school with. But somehow he managed to find him and cut off his head. I had wondered why he'd asked which Marcus was picking on me. I never thought he'd do anything like this. Usually when I see one of Steve's severed heads I get sick. My stomach starts to cramp like I have diarrhea and then I fight back the urge to throw up. Not this time, though. I'm kinda glad that he killed Marcus. I'm glad that he used something to cut his head off. It's really the nicest thing that anyone's ever done for me.

I look at David. David looks at me. "Are you scared?" I ask him.

He starts to shake. "What is this?"

"It's like the movie," I tell him. "It's just like *Headless*."

"Is this a joke?" he asks me. He's begging. He wants it to be a joke. "Are you fucking with me? Please tell me you're fucking with me."

"I'm not fucking with you," I say. "Steve kills people all the time."

"You're lying." But he knows I'm not.

"I thought you'd be scared," I tell him. "Are you?"

"Yes." He says it like it's hard for him to speak. He falls down onto his butt and pulls his knees into his chest. "I'm scared, Marty. You win."

"Look at it." I'm being mean now. Just like he was to me.

"No." David closes his eyes tight. "I just want to go home."

"Look at it," I tell him again.

"No!" he shouts.

"Be quiet. Steve might be home by now."

David looks at the bedroom door. His eyes are really wide. "Do you think he'll kill me if he knows that we found the head?"

I shrug my shoulders. "I don't know."

"I want to go home," he says. "I want to call my parents."

"You can't tell anyone about this," I say. "If you do, I'll tell Steve that you know."

Tears are falling down his cheeks. "You wouldn't do that, would you?"

"You hate me," I say. "Why wouldn't I?"

"You wouldn't tell Steve that I know, would you?" He's terrified. He's scared. That's exactly what he gets for being mean to me. I'm glad that he's worried about Steve. It makes me feel better about myself that I've scared David so bad. After the way he treated me tonight he deserves this and more. I want to make it worse. I want him to be really scared. Really, really scared.

"I'm going to tell Steve," I say. I'm smiling. I try to sound like I'm being serious. "I'm going to tell Steve you know about the heads."

"Don't do that," he cries. "Please. I'm sorry."

"You know why Steve did this?"

"Please don't." David can't stop crying. He just can't. He's too scared.

"Because Marcus punched me in the stomach and told everyone that I have a small penis," I tell him. "Because Marcus was picking on me."

"I won't pick on you. I promise," David cries. He just cries and cries. "I won't tell anyone about the heads. I won't do anything you don't want me to."

"You punched me," I say. "You punched me just like Marcus did."

"I won't do it again," David says. He's sobbing now. It makes it hard for him to breathe. I feel good about myself. I feel good because I'm getting even.

"Good," I say.

David covers his mouth. "I'm going to be sick."

"Go to the bathroom," I tell him. "Don't throw up in here."

He stands up and runs out of the room. I hear the bathroom door shut. Then I hear him getting sick in the toilet. It's echoing through the whole house. I'm sure my parents are going to hear it. I know they're going to wake up and see who's sick. They're not the kind of parents to let someone get sick without trying to help them. I quickly run out into the hallway. Mom's coming out of her bedroom. She doesn't see me coming out of Steve's bedroom. She knocks on the bathroom door.

"Are you okay?" she asks. "Who's in there?"

"Me," I hear David say. He sounds pretty sick. He throws up again.

"Do you want me to come in?" she asks.

"I want my mom," he says. He's still crying. "Can you call my mom?"

"Sure," she says. "I'll be right back."

She goes back into her bedroom and closes the door. I go into my bedroom and turn on the TV. I want her to think that David got sick from watching a hor-

ror movie. She knows that's what we do when he spends the night so she probably won't think anything's wrong. I can't let her know that we were in Steve's
bedroom. She can't know about the severed heads. After I make everything look
normal, I go back into the hallway. I need to straighten Steve's bedroom before
he gets home. I need to make sure everything looks normal before Mom comes
out of her bedroom.

But when I go into the hallway, Steve's bedroom door is closed.

"Oh my God," I say.

I'm too late.

Steve's already back.

"Oh my God," I say again. Nobody's around to hear me. His door is closed.
Music is coming from inside his bedroom. He knows that I know about his
hobby. He knows that I know about his heads. What's worse is that he knows
that David knows, too. I start to panic. My hands start to shake really bad.

I don't know what to do.

Mom comes out of her bedroom. She's wearing regular clothes instead of her
nightgown. "They're on their way," she tells the bathroom door. I can still hear
David throwing up. "Do you want me to come in there?"

"No," he tells her. "I'm okay."

But he's not okay. He's seen a severed head. He's not okay. I remember the
first time I saw one. I did the exact same thing. I couldn't stop crying and I
couldn't stop throwing up. I was scared and worried and I felt like the world was
coming to an end. I just hope Steve won't hurt me. Why would he? I'm his little
brother. He's my big brother. It's David that has to worry. David has to worry
about what Steve will do to him now that he knows. I might have to worry, too.
Nobody is safe.

Mom sees me standing in the hallway. "What happened?"

"I don't know," I tell her. "We were watching a movie and he just started feeling sick. Then he started throwing up."

"Get his stuff together," she says. "His parents are on their way."

I go into the bedroom and get his stuff together. I pack away his pencils and
paper for the comic book. I pack away the movies he brought over for us to
watch. I know this will be the last time that David spends the night. There's no
way that he'll want to come over after what happened tonight. He'll probably
avoid me at school, too. I've lost my friend. My best friend. When I go back to
school on Monday I won't have anyone to talk to. I won't have anyone. Nobody.

I bring David's backpack out into the hallway and set it in front of the stairs.
"Is he gonna be okay?" I ask Mom. "He sounds pretty bad."

"I don't know," she tells me.

The bathroom door opens and David steps out. His face is white and he's sweating like crazy. Little chunks of puke stick to his lips. He looks like he's just seen a ghost. Mom puts her arm around his shoulder and leads him downstairs. I pick up his backpack and follow them down. I don't say anything to David. David doesn't say anything to me. It's probably better that way.

"Are you okay?" Mom asks him.

"I'm sick," he says.

"I know that. But are you done throwing up?" She's really worried.

"I'm sick." That's all he can say.

After a few minutes his parents show up. They knock on the door and Mom answers it. She gives David his backpack and he leaves without saying goodbye to me. I expected that. Mom talks to David's mom for a second and then closes the front door. After locking it, she turns to me with a worried look on her face.

"I hope he didn't bring something home from school," she says.

"Like what?" I don't know what she means.

"Like a virus or something," she explains. "The last thing I need right now is for you to get sick. Then your Dad will get sick and then I'll get sick."

"What about Steve?" I ask.

She gives me a weird look. "What about Steve?"

"Aren't you worried he'll get sick, too?"

"Don't worry about Steve," she tells me. "He's never around to catch anything."

But he's around right now.

Upstairs.

With Marcus' head in the bag.

Oh my God.

Steve knows that I know.

Steve knows.

Oh my God.

CHAPTER 12

▼

MOVIES

I can't sleep.

All I can think about is Steve and Marcus.

How did he know where to find Marcus? Steve doesn't know any of the kids I go to school with. He doesn't even know what Marcus looks like. I guess he found him because I told him his full name. I just don't know how he did it. And what do I do now that Steve knows I've seen his heads? Will he kill me, too? I've got too many questions. All of them are going through my head at the same time. I can't sleep. All I can do is lay on my back in my bed and stare at the posters on my ceiling. I wish I'd never shown David that head. I wish things were different.

And what about Marcus? Where was he killed? Did Steve drag him out of his house while he was sleeping? I can't picture that part in my head. All I can see is Marcus' head in that bowling ball bag. All I can see are his eyes looking up at nothing. I feel bad for Marcus but I don't feel bad for him. Does that make sense? I hate it that someone else had to die but I'm glad it was Marcus. I don't like saying that he deserved it but deep down I think he probably did.

David isn't my friend anymore. I don't have anyone to talk to at school now. What will I do? Who will I hang out with at recess? Even though I talk to some of the kids in my QUEST class, it's not the same. They don't like horror movies and they don't draw comic books with lots of violence and blood. They don't really understand me. Everyone thinks that I tried to kiss Marcus after he looked at my penis. Everyone thinks I'm gay. I don't want to go back to school ever again. I want to be home schooled like that kid down the street. I just want to be left alone.

I don't sleep at all.

I'm even awake when Mom goes to work. She hates working on Saturdays but sometimes her boss makes her. You don't bother Mom when she's getting ready for work on Saturdays. She prefers to be left alone. I guess she's angry that she has to work and she doesn't want to take it out on us. Even Dad stays in bed while she gets ready. I smell coffee brewing downstairs. I smell something cooking in the microwave. Mom's making herself breakfast. I hear her put something in a plastic bag and then I hear her leave. Then the house is quiet. Really quiet.

Around ten I hear Steve's bedroom door open. He closes it and walks to my bedroom door. I hold my breath and pray that he doesn't come in. He doesn't. Instead, I hear him run his hand across the door. A few seconds later I hear him go downstairs. The front door opens, shuts, and I hear Steve walk to his car. After I hear him drive away I get out of bed and walk to my door. What did he do? Why did he rub it?

Stuck to my bedroom door is a small note written on yellow legal paper. It's the kind that comes in a pad. Steve ripped a piece in half and wrote something on it. It says, "We'll talk tonight." My heart stops. I feel like I'm going to choke. He knows that I know. And he wants to talk to me about it. I don't want to talk to Steve about his heads. I want to pretend as if nothing ever happened. I just hope that David doesn't tell his parents about the severed head in Steve's closet. But I don't think he will. My threats scared him pretty bad last night. If he does tell his parents about the head, then I'll tell Steve what happened. I'll tell him it was all David's fault.

I will not be a severed head in a bowling ball bag.

I pull the note off my door and wad it up. Dad comes out his bedroom. His hair is messy and his eyes are half open. It takes Dad at least two hours to wake up. He gives me a little smile as he goes into the bathroom and shuts the door. The shower starts up. Dad always starts off the day with a really hot shower. He says it helps him wake up and prepares him for the day. I'm the same way. If I don't get a shower in the morning then I feel like the whole day is screwed up. I really need a shower this morning. I want to wash off this nasty feeling I have. I'm going to need lots of soap.

I go down to the kitchen and fix myself a bowl of cereal. It's the kind with different marshmallow shapes. I know that I'm probably too old for a kid's cereal but it tastes really good. I sit down at the table and watch Saturday morning cartoons while Dad gets his shower. He's in there for a long time. When he finally comes downstairs he's dressed in a T-shirt and blue jeans. He only wears blue jeans on the weekends. Most of the time he wears slacks and a button-down shirt and a tie.

"Still wanna see a movie today?" he asks. He yawns as he says it. It makes his voice sound really weird. "I'll take you if you wanna go."

"Sure," I tell him. "Which one?"

"I'll grab the paper," he says. He walks to the front door.

"It's already in the kitchen," I say. "I think Mom already brought it in."

He stops right before he opens the front door. "She never brings it in."

I shrug my shoulders. "I dunno. It's in the kitchen. Maybe Steve brought it in."

Dad gives me a look when I say Steve's name. It's like he doesn't want me to say it in front of him. He's probably still mad at him over the fight they had last night. Sometimes I think my parents have given up on Steve. I'm surprised they haven't kicked him out of the house for good. Most parents won't put up with someone who acts like that, even if it is their first kid. But my parents can be pretty understanding sometimes. Steve hates them with a passion. They let him stay in their house even though he's rude to them all the time. Parents are weird. I don't think they would let a complete stranger treat them the way Steve treats them.

I keep eating and watching cartoons. Dad goes into the kitchen and gets the paper. He also gets a cup of coffee. Then he sits down at the table with me and flips to the movie section of the newspaper. He yawns again and takes little sips of his coffee while he reads. I just watch cartoons and eat around some of hard marshmallows in my cereal. It's pretty stale but I don't care. It still tastes pretty good. And you can't watch Saturday morning cartoons without cereal.

"What about *Dawn Of The Dead*?" he asks.

"Will Mom be mad if you take me to that one?" I ask.

"Mom's not here," he says.

He has a very good point. "That's fine with me."

"We'll go to the matinee," he tells me. "You might want to get a shower after you're done eating. We'll leave pretty soon."

"Okay," I tell him. You don't have to tell me twice when it comes to stuff like that. I like going to the movies early so I can get a really good seat.

I finish eating while Dad reads the paper. I try to sneak peeks at the news stories to see if there's anything about Marcus in there. I don't see anything. But I can't really get a good look at it because of the way Dad's reading it. He's got one of his arms blocking most of the words. He's also got his coffee cup sitting on another part of it. Steve better hope that the newspaper doesn't start covering his murders. I wonder how he hides the bodies? I wonder what he does with the rest of them?

I don't want to think about that right now.

After I'm done with my cereal, I go into the kitchen and put my dirty dishes in the sink. Then I go upstairs and turn on the shower. Dad didn't leave me much hot water. That's nothing new. Dad likes to stay in the shower until every last drop of hot water is gone. I quickly wash up and get out before it gets really cold. It takes me about fifteen minutes to dry off and get dressed. When I'm done I go back downstairs. Dad's still reading the paper. He's reading the comics. He never laughs at them but he reads them anyway. I don't understand him sometimes.

"Has Steve already left?" he asks me.

"I think so," I tell him. I know he's already gone but I don't want it to look like I keep tabs on him all the time. That would seem strange.

"He parked that goddamn car in the driveway again," he tells me. I don't know why he's telling me about it. There's nothing I can do to stop him. "There's oil all over the place. If you see him today, tell him to keep that thing on the street."

"Okay," I say. I'll see him tonight.

Tonight.

Oh my God.

"You okay?" Dad asks. "You look like you're gonna cry."

"I'm okay," I lie. "Just allergies."

"Well, grab your coat," he tells me. "It's supposed to be chilly today."

On our way out of the house, I grab my coat from the hook near the door. Then we get inside Dad's truck and back out of the driveway. Our house looks really small for some reason. It's hard to believe horrible things are going on behind those walls. It's weird to think that such a normal looking place is the home of a crazed psychopath. A psychopath that uses horror movies as a guideline for his murders. That's like the plot for every other horror movie at the video store. Steve is a cliché. He probably thinks he's special but he's really just another bad horror movie.

It takes us about twenty minutes to get to the movie theater. We always go to the really big one on the other side of town. It has really cool seats so that the person in front of you doesn't block the screen. It also has cup holders for your drink built right into the arm rest. There are all sorts of giant movie posters on the walls and hanging from the ceiling. Neon lights make everything look like Las Vegas.

I've never been to Las Vegas but I know what it looks like. This theater is my favorite. I love seeing movies in this place. It's just a lot of fun.

Dad buys the tickets and waits in line to get buttered popcorn and a really big Coke. I wait near the arcade. Some older kids are playing a shooting game. I stand around and watch since I don't have any quarters to spend on anything. It doesn't take long for Dad to get our food. After some guy tears our tickets and tells us where to go we walk down a long hallway filled with doors. The door we want is towards the very back. That's because *Dawn Of The Dead* has been out for a few weeks. The newer movies are closer to the front of the theater.

We find good seats right in the middle of the room. The big screen is right in front of us. Not too high and not too low. It's just right. Dad starts eating popcorn right away. I like to save it for the movie. Dad doesn't seem to care when he eats it. There's nobody else in the theater with us. Advertisements play on the screen. I always ignore them. I see enough commercials on TV. Watching them in a big theater just seems stupid.

"What happened to David last night?" Dad asks. He has a mouthful of popcorn.

"He got sick," I tell him. That's all I say.

"You two okay?" he asks.

I shake my head. I don't know what else to say.

"You two fighting?" Dad asks. He's stopped eating his popcorn.

"He said he didn't want to be my friend anymore," I say. "It's because he gets picked on for being my friend. So he doesn't want to hang out with me."

"That's bullshit," Dad says. "That kid's no good, anyway."

I don't say anything. I feel like I'm going to be sick.

"What time is it?" I want to change the subject.

Dad checks his watch. "We've got about ten minutes until it starts."

I sigh. This isn't much fun.

Everything is building up inside of me. School is bothering me. Steve is bothering me. David is bothering me. Everything is bothering me. Usually I can forget everything when I'm watching a movie in a theater. I can't do that today. There's too much on my mind. It won't let me relax and enjoy myself. I think Dad can sense that I'm not in a really good mood. He keeps giving me a look like he's not sure what I am. Like I've got something growing out of my forehead. I want to tell him everything just to get it off my chest. But I know better than to spill my guts.

My stomach starts to hurt. I groan.

"You okay?" he asks. He's still eating popcorn like crazy.

"I feel sick," I tell him. I clutch my stomach. It's really uncomfortable.

"Hurry and go to the bathroom," he tells me. He looks at his watch again. "You've got about eight minutes until the movie starts."

I don't want to miss the previews. Sometimes they're the best part about going to the movies. But I feel like I might mess my pants if I don't go to the bathroom. I nod my head and quickly make my way out of the theater and down the hallway. Once I'm inside the bathroom, I go into a stall and pull down my pants and underwear. My bowel movement is watery and it burns my butt hole. I hope that nobody else can hear me use the bathroom. I hope they can't smell it, either.

While I'm trying to flush everything down the toilet, someone comes into the bathroom. I can hear their feet tap-tap-tap across the tile floor. But they don't stop at the urinals and they don't stop at the sinks. Whoever it is makes their way to my stall and stands right in front of it. I feel like I'm at school again. I expect someone to start crawling under the stall to get a look at my little penis. I don't flush the toilet again. There's still a loose turd floating in the bowl.

There's a knock on the stall door.

"I'm in here," I tell the person. "Go to another stall, please."

They knock again.

"I'm in here," I say. I try to sound irritated. "Go away, please."

They knock again.

"Go away!" I yell. I'm getting scared.

"I know you're in there," a familiar voice says. "Open the stall."

Oh my God.

It's Steve.

"Steve?" I ask.

"Open the stall, Marty," he says. He sounds like he means business. "Open it or I'll kick it open. Either way."

I take a few steps back. "I'm using the bathroom."

"Bullshit," he snaps. "Open the fucking door, Marty. Open it."

I flush the toilet. "Hold on."

But he doesn't hold on. He kicks the stall door, snapping the lock. The door swings open. Steve's standing there, dressed in all black, his hands balled up into fists. He looks like he's going to beat me up. I back as far away from him as I can go. He enters the stall and pushes the door shut. Since he broke the lock it won't stay put.

"Did you tell Dad?" he asks. His eyes are wide. He's really angry.

"Did I tell him what?" I ask.

"Don't fucking play stupid with me," he says. Steve grabs me by the shirt and slings me out of the stall. I stumble against the wall.

"I'm not playing stupid," I tell him. "I haven't said anything to Dad."

He gets right in my face. His breath smells horrible. "Don't you dare say anything to Dad about what you saw last night."

"I wouldn't do that," I say. I can't stop shaking.

Steve slaps me across the face. "I'm not fucking around with you, Marty. Say one word to Dad about what you saw and you're dead."

I close my eyes and start to cry.

"Did you hear me? You'll be dead." Steve keeps staring right at me. "And what about David? Did he see it, too?"

"Yes," I tell him. It's hard to talk. "But I warned him."

"What?"

"I told him you'd kill him if he told anyone," I say. "That's why he left early last night. He was scared to death. He won't tell anybody anything."

"If he does, he's dead," Steve says. "I'm not fucking around."

"I know you're not," I tell him. "I know you're serious."

"I can't fucking believe this," he says. He finally takes a few steps away. He runs his fingers through his hair. "I can't fucking believe this."

I don't say anything. I try to stop crying. I don't want Dad to know that I've been crying in the bathroom. Then he'll really wonder what's wrong. He'll wonder why I was crying in the bathroom and I'll have to make up something stupid. I can't tell him that Steve followed us here. I can't tell him about the heads or David or anything. I can't tell him anything. I need to stop crying.

Steve gets in my face again. He's got his finger pointed right at me. "You really fucked up, kiddo. Really fucked up."

"I'm sorry," I say. "I didn't mean to see it."

"How long have you known?" he asks.

I don't say anything. I just stand there and look at the floor.

He grabs me by my shirt and pulls me in close. "I'm not fucking around with you, Marty. How long have you known about this?"

Someone walks in the bathroom. It's one of the theater employees. He's wearing a purple shirt with the picture of a cartoon cat on it. He looks scared because of how Steve's acting. "Is there something wrong?" he asks.

Steve lets me go. "We're brothers."

The employee nods his head. He knows how brothers are.

"We're not done," Steve whispers to me. "We'll talk again tonight."

"Okay," I tell him. "I'm not going to say anything to Dad."

"You'd better not." He means it, too.

As he walks out of the bathroom, he gives the employee an evil look. The employee backs against the wall so that Steve has plenty of room. Once he's gone, the employee exhales and laughs nervously. He gives me a look and steps up to a urinal. I adjust my clothes and wipe away the tears from my cheeks. I'm pretty shaken up. I hope I don't look like a wimp.

"That guy's an asshole," the employee says. I can hear him peeing.

"He's my brother," I say.

"He's still an asshole," the employee tells me. "I gotta brother, too, and he's an asshole just like that guy. Always tryin' to act tough and shit."

I'll bet his brother is nothing like Steve. I'll bet his brother doesn't collect the heads of black women as a hobby. I wash my hands in the sink using pink liquid soap and dry off my hands using the hot air machine. After checking my face in the mirror, I head back to the theater. The previews have already started. Dad looks a little annoyed with me. I was gone longer than I planned.

"Where'd you go? China?" he asks.

"I had a loose bowel movement," I tell him.

Dad makes a face. "I really didn't need to know that."

"Sorry," I tell him.

We watch the movie in silence. It's pretty good, but I can't really enjoy it. There's too much on my mind. Steve must've been really worried that I'd tell Dad about his heads if he followed us all the way to the theater. And what else does he want to talk to me about? He's already threatened to kill me if I say anything to anyone about his hobby. What else is there to talk about? I don't want to hear anything else he has to say. I just want him to leave me alone. I wish I'd never looked in his closet. I wish I'd never learned his nasty little secret.

The violence in the movie gets under my skin.

What if Steve kills me next?

What am I gonna do?

What am I gonna do?

CHAPTER 13

▼

ANTICIPATION

I didn't enjoy the movie.

I don't enjoy lunch, either.

Dad keeps asking if something's wrong. Something is wrong. Very wrong. But I don't know how to tell him. What would happen if they knew Steve's secret? They'd probably call the police and have him arrested. Then he'd go to court, then to jail, and then someone would probably kill him while he slept in his cell. I've seen it happen in movies before. The other prisoners would be really mean because Steve is a very handsome guy. He doesn't look like some psychopath who lops off heads when he feels the need to. He looks like you and me.

We eat at Friday's. I have a chicken sandwich. Dad gets some sort of steak. It's thick and meaty and bloody. He likes his meat rare. I can't eat rare meat. It has to be cooked all the way if I'm going to eat it. All of that blood reminds me of too many things. Things I've seen in horror movies. Things I've seen on the news. Things I've seen in our house. My favorite teacher Ms. Embry says that eating meat is wrong. She taught us about slaughterhouses and how cows are treated before they are turned into food. Lots of parents complained about it. Mine did, too.

I take a little bite of my sandwich. Then I dip one of my steak fries in ketchup and stick it in my mouth. Dad just looks at me.

"Is this about David?" he asks.

I shrug. "A little bit."

"Is this about school?" he asks.

I shrug again. "I don't want to talk about it."

Dad looks upset. "Talking about it will help you feel better."

"I don't want to talk about it," I tell him again. I mean business this time. I try to sound like I mean business so he won't bother me about it.

Dad holds up his hands. "I give up."

He really didn't try that hard.

We eat the rest of our lunch in complete silence.

On the way home we drop off the videos that I rented the other day. I don't rent anything else because Dad doesn't offer. I don't like asking Dad for things. Whenever you ask him for something he rolls his eyes and acts like he's really upset. He makes everything a big deal. So I don't ask Dad for anything unless Mom makes me. Usually she makes all of the decisions. I put the videos in the return slot and get back in the truck. Dad doesn't say a word.

My belly's upset. I groan a little.

"Are you all right?" Dad asks. We're at a stoplight. He looks at me like he's afraid I might throw up in his truck.

"My belly hurts," I tell him.

"Was it the food?" he asks. He's still trying to get me to talk. Dad isn't very good at being a dad sometimes so I can usually figure out what he's trying to do.

"Yeah," I tell him.

"I'm surprised you ate enough to make you sick," he says. This is what Mom calls a "snotty remark." I hate snotty remarks.

I don't say anything. I just groan again.

"Well, try not to get sick in the truck," he tells me. The light turns green. We drive off down the street. "Let me know if you need me to pull over."

"I'll be okay," I tell him. "Don't worry about your truck."

Dad gives me a mean look. "I'm not worried about the truck, Marty."

Yeah, right. That's the biggest lie I've ever heard.

We pull into the driveway and Dad turns off the truck. He just sits there and looks at me for a minute. Then he gets out of the truck without saying anything. Instead of helping me inside, he unlocks the front door, goes inside, and shuts it behind him. I'm left alone inside the truck. I've never felt so lonely. When your Dad doesn't seem to care about you it can make you feel really sad. I feel really, really sad. I try not to cry as I go inside the house. I don't want him to see me cry.

Dad's coat is hanging on the hook next to the front door. \I hang mine right next to his. If I don't then Mom might yell at me. I don't always remember to hang up my coat when I get home. Usually I just throw it on the floor somewhere. This makes Mom really mad. Since I don't like it when Mom's mad at me I try to remember to hang it up. It falls off the hook twice before it finally stays up there. We really need a new place to hang our coats. The hooks near the door have too many coats on them.

The TV's on some kind of sports show. Dad's sitting in his recliner. He's already got a beer in his hand. Dad doesn't drink during the week but he makes up for it on the weekends. He drinks and drinks and drinks until he passes out in his chair. One time he let me taste his beer. It was the nastiest thing I've ever tasted. I can't believe people actually want to drink it. They spend their money on it. They share it with their friends. That stuff is just plain nasty.

"Your Mom will be home soon," he tells me. I don't know why but he does.

"What's for dinner?" I ask. I don't know why I ask because I really don't feel like eating. But I ask it anyway. It's a stupid question.

"I don't know," Dad snaps. "I'm not the one who makes it."

He's in no mood to talk. I quickly climb the stairs.

Steve's bedroom door is closed. It's also locked. I know this because I try the knob. I don't really want to go inside, though. Not anymore. I'm already in big trouble as it is. He knows that I know about those heads. He's going to talk to me at some point tonight about it. He'll probably try to threaten me or make me look at Marcus' severed head while he explains what he's going to do to me if I tell anyone about his secret. That's one thing that Steve doesn't have to worry about. I'll never tell anyone about what I've seen. I saw what it did to David. Normal people can't handle this sort of horror. It's too much for them to handle. They'd puke if they saw it.

I guess that makes me unusual.

I guess that makes me a freak.

I guess everyone at school was right about me.

I go into my bedroom and close the door all the way. That means that I don't want to be disturbed unless it's time for dinner. I turn off all the lights and pull my dark blue curtains shut. Only a little sunlight gets in through the middle. I lay down on my bed, flat on my back, and stare up at the posters on my ceiling. I wish I was older. I wish I was either drawing comic books or making movies. I wish I didn't live next door to Steve anymore. I wish I didn't have to go to school Monday.

The whole thing is really my fault. I was the one who was snooping around my brother's bedroom looking for secrets. I was the one who unzipped that bowling ball bag and found the heads. I was the one who kept coming back day after day to see if he had something new in there. It's my fault. I wish I could go back in time like in *Back To The Future* so that I could tell myself not to go into Steve's bedroom. I'd tell myself that staying away from his closet would make my life easier. I might not even have a life after Steve gets done with me tonight.

Oh my God.

I might be dead by tomorrow morning.

I curl into a ball and start to cry. I can't help it. I'm really scared right now. All I can see in my head is Steve killing me with a machete. Just like that stupid movie *Headless*. Why did I watch that movie? Why did I make David watch that movie? Why did I show him Steve's secret? The only thing I'm really not sorry about is Marcus. He deserved getting his head cut off. I'm glad he's dead. That way he won't be able to pick on me in school anymore. This is a good thing.

Torture scenes are always the scariest in horror movies. Those nasty scenes where the killer just plays around with his victim before finally killing them. Sometimes they slash at them with their knives. Sometimes they string them up and do horrible things to them. And sometimes they just cut off body parts one at a time. Those scenes always make me nervous. What if someone did that to you? That would be one of the worst ways to die. I wonder if Steve does all that stuff?

I don't know how long I cry.

After a while I hear the front door open.

Mom's home.

I can hear her and Dad talking about something downstairs. Then she climbs the stairs and knocks on my bedroom door. Dad must have told her about this afternoon. He knows that something's wrong with me so he told Mom about it. And when Mom knows that there might be something wrong with me she wants to talk about it. That's why she's knocking on my door right now. Dad told her about this afternoon. She's concerned and worried about me. I'd be worried, too.

"It's me," she says through the door. "Can I come in?"

I wipe off my cheeks with the back of my hand. "Yeah," I say. "Come in."

She slowly opens the door. When she sees that I've been crying she makes a really sad face. "Are you okay, sweetie? You look like you've had a bad day."

"David's not my friend anymore," I tell her. The tears start coming again. It's really upsetting. "He said that it's too much for him."

"Too much for him?" she asks. "What does that mean?"

Mom sits down on the edge of the bed and rubs my leg. It's comforting. "He says that he gets picked on at school for being my friend. It's too much for him. I guess they call him names for hanging out with me all the time."

"And he said he doesn't want to be your friend anymore?" she asks.

"Yeah," I tell her. "We had a fight about it last night. That's why he got sick and went home. I guess he didn't really want to be here."

"He seemed fine when he got here," she says.

"I thought so, too," I say. "But I guess he was faking it."

We don't say anything for a long time.

"Do you want to come downstairs and get some dinner? Dad said you didn't eat very much this afternoon." Did he tell her everything?

"I'm not very hungry," I tell her. "Maybe later."

"I brought home KFC," she says. She fakes a big smile. "You want some?"

My stomach hurts. "I don't think so. I don't feel good."

"Well, I'll save you some," she says. She pats me on the leg. "You want me to leave you alone for a little while? Let you rest?"

"Yeah," I tell her. "Is that okay?"

"It's okay," she says. "Can I come up later and check on you?"

I smile. It's a real smile. "Okay."

"Okay," she says. She's smiling, too. "I'll check on you later."

Mom pats me on the leg again and stands up. "You want some light in here? I could turn on one of the lamps for you."

"No," I say. "I want it dark."

She nods. She knows what kind of mood I'm in. Sometimes I just want to be left alone. It's nice to lay in a dark room without any sound or light. You can just think about things without other stuff getting in the way. When I'm really nervous about something this is one of the only ways I know of to help me calm down. The other way is to play *Morrowind* for hours and hours. But playing *Morrowind* right now will make me think about Steve. He's the last person I want to think about right now. I just want to lay in the dark and think about imaginary things.

Mom closes the door on her way out. I curl back up and look at the wall. There's a poster from the *Morrowind* game that came with it. It's a map of the whole island where the game takes place. I never look at it since there's a map you can look at while playing the game. I just thought it might look good hanging on the wall. I really like *Morrowind*. It's one of those games you can play for hours and hours and not do the same thing twice. I like that. It helps me stop thinking of bad things.

Downstairs I can hear Mom and Dad getting plates and silverware from the cabinets and drawers in the kitchen. They're pretty loud. Dad laughs about something and Mom does, too. They're probably watching some kind of stupid sitcom on TV. I don't think I like my parents too much. They're nice people but they don't seem to know anything. They should know that Steve is doing something wrong. They should pay more attention to what's happening in their own house. People talk about bad parents all the time on the news. It seems like they're everywhere.

I love them.

I hate them.

I can't figure out which one is stronger.

I lay on my bed until it gets dark outside. I can still hear my parents downstairs. They're still watching TV. It's turned up too loud. That's the way Dad likes to watch it. The only reason it's up so loud is because Dad's laugh is louder than the TV. When he laughs you can't hear the other jokes that are being told. I don't see how Mom watches TV with him every night. It would drive me crazy.

I think that waiting is the worst part of anything. I hate waiting when we have to give oral reports because I hate talking in front of the class. Waiting for Steve to talk to me is like watching a horror movie where the killer is creeping up behind someone you know is going to die. I just keep imagining what he's going to do to me for knowing his secret. Whenever I close my eyes I can hear that laugh and see those heads from his closet. It's all I can think about right now.

Around ten o'clock I hear the backdoor open. I hear it shut. Then I hear footsteps on the stairs. They're fast and heavy and they stop right in front of my bedroom door. I stop breathing. I don't move. Is he going to come in here now? Is he going to talk to me when Mom and Dad are awake? I thought this would happen late at night.

Instead of coming in, Steve goes to his bedroom and shuts the door.

Then I hear music playing through the wall.

I start breathing again. That was close. I wasn't ready for what Steve is going to say. I wonder if he's nervous? I'd be nervous if someone found out that I was killing a bunch of black people. I'd be really nervous that whoever knew about it would call the police and turn me in. Maybe I can use that against him. If he tries to beat me up or hold a knife up to my throat I might tell him that I'll call the police if hurts me. I'll call the police and he'll be murdered in prison. That would make me nervous. I just hope Steve is nervous. I need him to be nervous, too.

I doze until Mom knocks on my bedroom door again.

"Come in," I say.

She opens the door a little and sticks her head in. "We're going to bed, sweetie."

"Okay," I tell her.

"There's still some chicken downstairs if you want a midnight snack," she says. "All you have to do is throw it in the microwave."

"Okay," I tell her again. I just want to be left alone.

"I'll wake you up around seven for church," she says.

I forgot about church. "I don't feel like going to church."

Mom makes a stern face. "You're going to church, Marty. It'll make you feel better." That's a big lie.

She doesn't really know anything about church. The little country church that we go to is about half-an-hour outside of town. It's the one Mom went to when she was growing up on the farm. Lots of farmers and their families go there. My uncles and aunts and cousins on my mom's side go there. I hate it more than anything. I hate it more than school. Even the kids in my Sunday School class are mean to me. They all go to the same school and know the same people. They have stuff to talk about before the lesson begins. I don't know anyone. I'm an outsider.

"But I don't feel good," I tell her. I'm whining now. I really don't want to go. When things get tough, I almost always start to whine.

"Enough," she snaps. "You're going and that's final."

"Whatever," I say. I turn away from her. "Close the door."

Mom sighs. Then she shuts the door.

God I hate church.

It takes me forever to finally fall asleep. All I can think about are church clothes and Sunday School and those spoiled little farmer's kids that always make fun of me. I hate them all. When I get older I'm never going back to church. Never. It's useless. Church is supposed to be about Jesus and God and people getting along. All the people do at church is talk about people behind their backs and complain when something goes wrong. And it seems like there's always something wrong at church. I hate it. I would rather be at school than at church.

It's because of the people at church that I don't believe in God.

God wouldn't let one of his children be treated this way. Especially me. I'm always good at church. I'm always quiet. And I'm always the one who gets treated bad. So how can I believe in God? How can I believe He's good when His church is so bad?

I'm thinking about all this as I fall asleep.

But I'm not asleep for long.

Around two in the morning I hear my bedroom door open. I hear it shut. I hear the tap-tap-tap of feet across the hardwood floor. Someone's in my bedroom. Steve's in my bedroom. I hear him walk to the side of my bed. Then I don't hear anything. Nothing. Just the buzz of silence in my ears. And just when I think I imagined the whole thing there's a blinding light in my eyes. He's shining a flashlight directly in my face. I can't see anything. Just bright white light.

"Okay, kiddo," he says. "How much do you know?"

I take a breath.

How much do I know?

CHAPTER 14

▼

MOTIVES

Steve won't turn off the flashlight.

"I don't feel good, Steve," I tell him. "Leave me alone."

"I need to know, Marty. How much do you know?" He's still holding that flashlight in my face. I turn away from him. "Tell me."

I'm scared. I'm nervous. This is the thing I've been dreading for as long as I've known about the heads. A killer is standing over my bed with a flashlight in my face. A killer wants to know how much I know about his hobby. A psychopath wants me to talk to him. I don't know what to say. I don't know what to do. All I know is that his flashlight is giving me a headache. I hope that turning away from him will make him leave my room. It doesn't. It only irritates him.

"Turn over," he says. "Look at me."

"No," I snap. "Get away from me."

Steve takes a step back. "What did you just say to me?"

I sit up. I'm angry. I'm scared. I'm running off at the mouth again. "I said get away from me, Steve. You scare me."

"Why did you look in my closet?" he asks.

I don't say anything.

"Why did you do it?" He sounds like he honestly wants to know.

"I don't know," I tell him. "I'm nosy. I look through everybody's stuff. I look at Dad's dirty magazines and Mom's old love letters. I didn't think you'd have body parts in your closet, Steve. I thought you might have some cool stuff in there."

He doesn't say anything. I lay on my back and look at the posters on my ceiling. They aren't helping me calm down. Steve turns off the flashlight and sits down on the edge of my bed. We're in the dark now. Steve doesn't act like he wants to kill me. He's acting like the old Steve again. I like the old Steve. We used to play video games together. We used to watch movies together. It seems like such a long time ago. I haven't seen the old Steve in a long time.

"Why'd you do it, Marty," he says. He sounds sad. "Why?"

"I don't know," I tell him again. "I'm sorry."

He sighs. "I know you are."

"I really am."

"I know you are," he says again.

I take a deep breath. "Are you going to kill me?"

Steve laughs. He doesn't say anything else.

"Are you going to kill me?" I ask again. I need to know.

I hear him scratch his head. He's thinking about it. "Are you going to tell anyone, Marty? Have you told anyone?"

"Just David," I tell him. "Are you going to kill me?"

He ignores my question. "That's right. David knows, too."

"Yeah," I say. "But I scared him into not saying anything to anybody."

"How'd you do that?" Steve asks.

"I told him that if he did you'd probably kill him," I tell him. "Am I right?"

"No, you're not," he says. "It's not like that."

"Then what's it like?" I ask. "Tell me. I want to know."

Steve's mood changes. I can feel it. He moves around on the bed a lot like he's really uncomfortable. He doesn't say anything for a long time. I don't say anything for a long time, either. We just sit in the dark. We sit in silence. I can hear cars going by outside. I can hear dogs barking in the neighborhood. Everything seems so normal outside. I want everything to be normal inside. I'd like to wake up. I wish this was nothing but a bad dream. A really bad dream.

"It's those niggers," Steve finally says. He sounds angry. Furious. I've never heard so much hatred in his voice before. "Those fucking niggers."

I hate the "N" word. Dad uses it sometimes. That's why I don't like talking to Dad about black people. I guess some of his racism rubbed off on Steve. I don't say anything to Steve about it. He's dead serious right now. I don't want to make him angry at me. No telling what he might do. Even though Mom and Dad are right next door I don't feel safe. He could strangle me without them hearing a sound. He could beat me to death with that flashlight. He could do anything he wants to do.

"You mean black people?" I finally say.

"No, I mean the fucking niggers!" he says. It's loud. Loud enough that Mom and Dad might hear if they're still awake. "They're infesting everything! They're everywhere! The fucking mall! The fucking government! I can't get away from them!" He takes a breath. A long, deep breath. "Don't you hate them, Marty?"

"No," I say. "I don't."

"What about Marcus?" he says. "That fucking nigger told everyone that you had a small dick. Then he fucking punched you in the stomach. How can you sit there and say that you don't hate them? They're nothing. They're dirt. Fucking dirt-ass niggers. I wish I could get rid of every last one of them."

I really don't know what to say. I've never heard anyone talk like this before.

"Why do you cut off their heads?" I ask. It's a dangerous question. It's a stupid question. I don't know how he'll respond.

"Answer me!" he snaps. Some of his spit flies on my face. I don't wipe it off. I'm too afraid to move. "Why don't you hate them?"

"I just don't," I say. "I don't."

Steve doesn't say anything. He shifts his butt on the edge of the bed. "Why do you do it, Steve?" I ask. "I want to know."

"To kill them off," he says. "To get to the root of the problem. The female niggers are the breeders. They carry the offspring. Without them the race can't continue to grow. If I can dig out the root, I can stop the infection."

He's not making sense. "What are you talking about?" I ask.

Steve takes in another long breath. I guess he's trying to gather his thoughts. This seems like a hard thing for him to do. "Without the women, the niggers can't have babies. Then the nigger guys will fuck each other like the nigger fags they really are. Who does most of the raping in prison? Niggers. They'll stick their nasty black dicks in anything. That's fine with me. Let 'em fuck each other in the ass. They can't have babies that way. They can't continue to infect the world that way."

He takes another breath. "It's the niggers, Marty. The goddamn niggers. They're the ones that pick on you at school. They're the ones that are rude to you at restaurants. They're the ones who rob and rape you. They're the ones who make this world a dangerous place to live. It's the niggers, Marty. Don't you understand? I'm not the problem. They're the problem.

"I'm eliminating the root of the infection by killing off their women. Once I'm done with them, I'll work on the guys. Because you know what? They'll try

to take our women, Marty. They'll fuck white women just the same as their nigger bitches. They'll stick their nasty nigger cocks in a white pussy and produce an
entire race of half-breed niggers that will steal our jobs and infiltrate our lives."
His whole body is shaking. I don't know why. "Do you understand?"

"Yes," I lie.

"I just need them to die," he says. He sounds tired. "It's all I can think about.
I need to dig out that fucking root. I need to make sure they don't ruin our
nation. Our world. Our planet. I want to fucking kill them all."

My head is spinning. All of this is too much to think about. My brother is a
head collecting racist. It's too much to think about. It's too much to handle. I
want to wash my face. I want to wash my ears. I feel dirty for listening to him.
But I have so many unanswered questions. I want to ask him each and every one.
I really do want to understand. I want to know who my big brother is.

"How did you find Marcus?" I ask.

"That was easy," he says. Then he laughs. "His whole nigger family is nothing
but a pack of fucking breeders. All they do is fuck. I went to school with one of
his brothers. I know the Sanders family very well." He laughs again. It's evil and
it makes my skin crawl. "I've already disinfected one of his sisters."

"Are you going to kill me?" I ask.

"Are you going to tell anyone about me?" he asks.

"No," I tell him. But I'm not sure yet. I don't know what he's really capable
of. Would he kill me if he needed to? I think he would. I think he'd crawl into
my bedroom while I was asleep and he'd cut my head off. There'd be blood
everywhere. I don't think he would care, though. He'd just laugh as he put my
head into his bowling ball bag.

"I wouldn't kill you, Marty," he tells me. He reaches out and touches my leg. I
feel like I'm going to be sick. "You're my little brother."

"What about Mom and Dad?" I ask.

Steve doesn't say anything. He pulls his hand away.

"What about Mom and Dad?" I ask again.

"That's a different story," he says.

"What do you mean?" I ask.

"I hate them, Marty," he says. "They hate me, too. They just don't understand
me. They don't understand that I don't want to go to college. That I'm happy
working at the factory. They act so disappointed in me. I don't know how much
longer I can take it." He rubs his forehead. He looks stressed out.

"Move out," I tell him.

"No way," he says. "Mom and Dad never go into my room. Never. I wouldn't have that kind of privacy in an apartment. Do you know that a landlord can come into one of his apartments anytime he feels like it? No way, man. No way. Too much risk."

We don't say anything for a long time.

Things have happened to Steve over the years. Things I don't understand. Why is he so angry? Why does he hate black people? How does cutting off a person's head keep you from doing it again? It seems like nonsense. It seems like a bad horror movie that someone filmed with their friends over a few weekends. Maybe I'm just too young to understand the changes that Steve has gone through.

A part of me is really glad that he killed Marcus, though. I think he deserved it. All Marcus did was pick on people and say stupid things during our lessons. He caused more problems than anyone else in class. I don't think he would have gone to college. I don't think he would have been anyone important. I feel bad for saying that but it's true. Some people aren't worth very much. Marcus was one of them.

I clear my throat. "Thank you for killing Marcus," I tell him.

"You're welcome." It sounds like he's smiling. "Anything for my little brother."

He's being so nice. So kind. Just like the old Steve. But he's not the old Steve. I guess the old Steve is dead. He's not around anymore. This is some kind of new Steve that just looks like the old one. Sounds like the old one. Smells like the old one. But his brain is different. His thoughts are messy. I've heard about people with mental illnesses before. There's always something about them on the news. Like the guy who shot all those cars on the highway with a sniper rifle. Something was wrong with that guy. Something is wrong with Steve, too.

"What about David?" he asks. "Can I trust him?"

"I don't know," I tell him. "We're not friends anymore."

"Why not?" His voice is cold.

"He gets picked on for being my friend," I say. "He said it makes going to school too hard for him. I guess I can understand that."

"If he says anything…" He stops himself. "You know what I have to do."

"I know," I tell him.

Steve stands up and turns on his flashlight. It's back in my face. "Stay out of my room," he tells me. "I'm not kidding about that."

"Okay," I say. I can't see him because I'm squinting. "Turn off that light."

"Are you gonna stay outta my room?" he asks.

"Yes!" I say. I mean business now. He's making my headache worse. "I won't go in there anymore. I've learned my lesson."

"Good." He turns off the flashlight. "Get some sleep."

Yeah, right.

When he opens the door I can see his outline in the doorway. He's just standing there. I think he's watching me. After a few seconds he goes into the hallway and closes the door. I'm all alone. In the dark. With my thoughts. I still don't know what to think. I feel dizzy. I never knew Steve was so angry towards black people. I never thought that anyone would think of black people as an infection. Even though Steve didn't hit me or threaten me or call me names, he scared me even worse with his thoughts and ideas. It's too much to think about. Too much.

I get off the bed and get undressed in the dark. I want to crawl under the covers. I want to be comfortable. I need to be comfortable. I still feel dizzy. It's like everything I ever knew about Steve has been taken away. Now there's this person I don't know in his place. What am I supposed to do? Am I supposed to call the cops on my own brother? My big brother? Should I go to Mom and Dad? And if they confront him, will he kill them? It's dangerous. Very dangerous. I could be killed. Mom and Dad could be killed. And more innocent people could be killed.

After crawling under the covers, I turn on my clock radio. The talk show I usually listen to has already gone off. They're playing some sort of jazz music instead. For the first time I really don't mind listening to it. It's calm and soothing and I like the way it makes me feel. I try to snuggle beneath the covers. Morning will be here too soon. So will church. I don't think I can put my trust in God tomorrow. Not with someone like Steve living next door. I'm confused. I'm sick. I'm dizzy.

Steve is a racist. Steve is a psychopath. Steve is a killer.

What am I going to do?

CHAPTER 15

▼

CHURCH

I still don't feel good when Mom wakes me up.

I've had a really hard week.

"I don't want to go," I tell her. I'm still really sleepy. I'm not really awake yet. "Are you really gonna make me go?"

"It's church, Marty," she says. She's irritated with me. "You have to go to church."

Mom is religious. Sometimes. She says a silent prayer before we eat dinner and says another one before she goes to bed. She used to make me say my prayers before I went to bed. I don't know why but she doesn't make me do that anymore. I guess she knows that I don't mean any of it. I'm just saying the words. If she had it her way I think we'd go to church on Wednesday nights, too. But she doesn't make me go on Wednesdays. She only makes me go on Sundays.

I hate going to church.

Dad doesn't go to church with us. Mom says that just because he doesn't go to church doesn't mean I'm not going. I don't think that's fair. Why is she making me go? I hate going to church. It's filled with snotty kids and old people and our stuck-up relatives who think they're better than everyone else. The only other time I see these relatives are on holidays like Thanksgiving and Christmas. My uncles aren't very nice and my aunts are even worse. Uncle Hank teaches one of the adult Sunday School classes. He never speaks to me when I see him. I guess he doesn't like me.

Today I've got too much on my mind to go to church and sing songs about Jesus. I have more important things to think about. Like Steve and his anger towards black people. There's also school to think about. And David. And Marcus. And all the rumors people are spreading about me. All those lies. My head feels like it might split open. That would be cool. Mom wouldn't make me go to church if my brains were spilling out onto the floor. I don't know, though. She might make me tape it up and go anyway. Mom really wants me to be religious.

"Get up," she says. I'm starting to fall back asleep. She shakes me hard. "I'm not going to tell you again. Get up and get dressed."

"I want to take a shower," I tell her. I feel dirty after talking to Steve last night. A hot shower might make me feel better.

"We don't have time," she tells me. "I've tried to wake you up three times already. We're gonna leave in about fifteen minutes."

"What about breakfast?" I can't believe she's going to make me go to church on an empty stomach. That's just not right.

"You should have thought about that earlier," she tells me. She's just being mean now. "Get up and get dressed, Marty. On the double."

I swing my legs out of the bed and stomp them on the floor. Mom glares at me and leaves the room so I can get dressed. I don't like to get dressed in front of other people. It makes me nervous. I open my closet and dig out my Sunday clothes. I've only got one pair of nice slacks and one white button-down shirt. After I'm dressed I get a red clip-on tie out of my dresser drawer and put it on. Then I put on my brown loafers. I look the same every Sunday.

I go into the bathroom and brush my hair and teeth. But not with the same brush, though. I use the hairbrush for my hair and the toothbrush for my teeth. Then I put on some of Dad's aftershave. I really like the way it smells. Mom doesn't like me to put any on but I don't care what she thinks today. I need to make myself feel better. If I look good then I might feel good. When I look in the mirror I don't feel any better, though. My hair won't stay down and I look like a zombie. There are these big black circles under my eyes. I should be eating brains in a cemetery.

"Come on!" Mom yells from downstairs. "Let's get going!"

I want to cuss so bad. I want to go downstairs and tell her that I don't believe in God or Jesus or anything they teach us in Sunday School. I want to tell her that her prayers are stupid because she's just talking to her hands. I want to tell her that she doesn't know anything because her oldest son hates black people and is trying to get rid of them all. I want to make her feel horrible. She doesn't understand anything. She doesn't know anything. I'm really mad at her right now.

"I'm coming!" I yell at the top of my voice. I'm really angry. I hate being bossed around. I hate being told what to do when it's something I really don't want to do. I spit into my hand and rub it through my hair. Nothing works. It's going to stick up anyway. Sometimes I really hate the way I look.

Mom's waiting for me downstairs. She's already got the front door open and everything. I stomp down the stairs and grab my coat from the hook. She gives me a mean look and we go outside. Steve's car's gone. It's always gone. I have no idea where he goes all the time. That's one of the things I forgot to ask him last night. There's lots of things I forgot to ask him. Too late for that now. There's no way I'm going to bring that stuff up again. I'm never going in Steve's room again and I'm never going to watch *Headless*, either. When I get home from church I'm going to put that tape in front of his bedroom door so he can put it away. I don't care if he knows I've seen the tape he uses for inspiration. I just don't care about anything right now.

I get into the mini-van and slam the door shut. "Quit stomping around and quit slamming stuff," Mom snaps. "I'm not kidding, Marty. You'd better start acting your age. What's gotten into you?"

"Leave me alone," I say. I'm not going to tell her anything. "I don't want to talk to you." I try to sound as mean as I can.

Mom gives me a look. It's the kind of look she gives Steve when he walks by her without saying anything. I wonder if she thinks I'm going to end up like Steve. She probably does. I don't care what she thinks. Going to church is ruining my weekend. Kids are going to pick on me just like they do at school and she doesn't care. I've told her what they say about me. She's seen the way they laugh when they walk past me. But she doesn't care. She's there for God and Jesus and the Holy Ghost.

We ride to church in silence. We don't even listen to the radio. I sit in my seat and behave. Mom can think I'm moping around if she wants to. She doesn't know how bad this week has been for me. She probably doesn't care, either. Asking about my day is just her being a mother. She's just doing her job. Well, I'm not going to play her games anymore. When she asks me about my day she'll get a fake answer. I'll lie right to her face. She can't help me. What does she care?

Our church is way out in the middle of nowhere. That's why farmers go to this church because it's close to their farms. The parking lot is nothing but grass. Mom pulls the mini-van into the grass and turns off the engine. Then she turns in her seat and looks at me. I think she might cry but I'm not sure. I wonder what she's thinking? I don't care what she's thinking. She's making me go to church. I hate church. I hate using bad words, but fuck church. Fuck God.

"Are you mad at me?" she asks.

"Yes," I say.

"Can I ask why?"

I point to the church.

"Because I'm making you go to church?" she asks.

"Yes!" I shout. "I hate church! The kids pick on me like they do at school! I can't believe you would make me go somewhere that makes me unhappy."

"But you need to go to church, Marty," she says.

"I hate church," I tell her. "And I hate God. He doesn't look after me."

Mom grabs my left arm and squeezes it tight. It really hurts. "Don't you ever say that," she snaps. "Do you understand me?"

"Let go," I say. I jerk my arm away from her. "Don't you tell me what to do."

"What's gotten into you, Marty? Is this about school?"

I start kicking the glove compartment over and over again. I just kick and kick and kick. "It's about everything, Mom! It's about school and David and Steve and church and everything!" I keep kicking the glove compartment.

"Stop kicking!" she shouts. "Stop acting like you're three!"

"Do you know how to be a mom?" I ask. Her eyes get wide. She's getting ready to cry. "Because you messed up Steve and you're messing up me."

"How dare you," she whispers. I don't think I've ever seen her so angry. "How dare you talk to me that way. I can't believe this."

"You're just mad because I'm telling the truth," I tell her. I want to make her hurt the way the kids hurt me. That way she'll understand what I'm going through. "How can you make me go to church when all the kids do is pick on me in Sunday School?"

"Kids pick on other kids, Marty. I got picked on in school," she says. She's trying to make me feel better. It's not working.

"You just don't get it," I say. I open the door and get out. Then I slam it shut. Mom tries to keep from crying. If she cries then her makeup will run down her face and she'll look like a fool. Maybe that's what I want. I want her to look like a fool.

Mom gets out of the mini-van and locks the door. We walk up to the front doors in silence. Standing at the entrance is Frank. He's an old man with no hair and thick glasses. His job is to greet everyone who comes into the church. He's one of the few people at church who's actually nice. He always shakes my hand.

"Hello young man," he says to me. He sticks out his right hand. I shake it. "How are you doing this morning? You look a little sad."

"I'm okay," I lie. He doesn't need to know about my problems.

He talks to my mom for a second but I don't pay attention. I'm looking inside the church. There are rows and rows of people in there. Almost all of them are old. I don't know why Mom keeps coming back to this church. I know she went here when she was little but it still doesn't make sense to me. Everyone is worried about everyone else. Nobody minds their own business. But I guess I really shouldn't talk, though. If I had minded my own business then I wouldn't know about Steve's heads. I wouldn't know how much he hates black people. I would be a normal kid.

We go into the church and sit down towards the back of the room. After a few minutes the preacher comes out and starts talking. His name is Donald. He's a fat guy with a big bald spot in the middle of his head. When he shakes my hand before we leave he's always sweating. I don't like the sound of his voice. I wish someone else was the preacher. Maybe someone who made the sermons fun to listen to. Someone who doesn't sound bored and stupid and tired.

My aunts and uncles and cousins sit on the other side of the room. They don't talk to us. They don't even look over at us. Mom usually talks to them outside after church is over. I never talk to them. My cousins are older than me. We don't have anything in common. They live on the other side of town and go to different schools and do different things. None of them seem to like me. Even during Christmas and Thanksgiving they don't seem to like me. That's fine. Whenever they come over during the holidays I just stay in my room and play video games.

Mom doesn't talk to me. I don't talk to her, either. I really don't have anything else to say. She doesn't understand me. I don't understand her. That's fine. I like being left alone. I have too much to think about. I'm stressed out. Maybe I need to start taking pills to help me calm down. I don't think that kids should be stressed out. Adults are the ones who should be stressed out. Not me. Not like this.

After everyone sings this stupid song about Jesus on a mountain, it's time to go to our Sunday School classes. I don't say anything to Mom as I stand up. I just get up, walk towards the back of the church, and open the door to the basement. That's where the kids' Sunday School classes are. In the basement. The dirty, stinky basement. My class is in the room towards the very back of the basement. I hate Sunday School. I hardly ever pay attention. There's nothing fun about it.

"Hey faggot," someone says behind me. It's Trevor. He's the one who usually picks on me. "Nice clip-on, geek. Real classy."

Trevor is older than me. He's in the sixth grade. I think he's been held back before because he seems older than most sixth graders I know. As he passes me he pushes me against the wall. I don't say anything. I don't do anything. I just let him push me around like everyone else does. My temper is starting to get bad, though. I picture in my head all of the nasty things I would do to him. I even picture cutting off his head like Steve does. I'd use a machete to cut it off. I'd kill him in front of his parents and tell them every mean thing he's ever said to me. That way they'd understand. They might even thank me for getting rid of him. Nobody should have a kid like Trevor.

I go into the classroom and sit down. All of the kids sit down at a long table in the center of the room. They snicker behind my back. Trevor must be making fun of me again. I try not to pay attention but it's hard not to. No telling what he's saying. I'm worried that he may have heard something about me from someone who goes to the same school as I do. He might know about Leroy and Marcus and their lies. Aren't people supposed to be nice to each other at church? I thought that was what God wanted. Maybe Jesus wasn't so nice after all.

The lesson isn't anything special. Just more stories from the Bible. Our teacher is a woman named Barbara. She's the preacher's wife. She's just as fat as her husband but her hair is really long and brown. I don't like her, either. I know she hears what the other kids say about me but she doesn't do anything about it. She just reads from the Bible and gives us our lesson. I'm always distracted by what the other kids are saying about me.

"Hey Marty," Trevor whispers. He's sitting across from me at our table. "Your clip-on is gay. You hear me? You're a fag."

I know Barbara hears him. She doesn't say anything.

I sit in silence for the entire lesson.

Our project for today is to take our favorite character from the Bible and draw a picture of them. Then beside the picture we're supposed to write what we like about them. I don't have a favorite character from the Bible. I've never really paid any attention to the stories. I don't know any of their names. Instead of a character from the Bible I draw a picture of Roach-Man. He's wearing his costume and you can see the skyline behind him. Barbara doesn't even look at the pictures when we turn them in. She just stacks them beside her big Bible and smiles at us.

As I'm leaving the classroom, Trevor shoves me against the wall. "I was talking to you, fag," he says. He's angry. I don't know why. I haven't done anything to him. "When I talk to you, faggot, you'd better listen to me."

I don't say anything.

Trevor shoves my head. It hits the wall.

"Say something, faggot," he says.

I don't know what's happening. Everything that's happened to me over the past week is driving me crazy. I'm angry. Angrier than I can ever remember being in my entire life. I'm angry at school. I'm angry at Steve. I'm angry at Mom. I'm angry at Dad. I'm angry at David. I'm angry at God. I'm angry at everyone. And I'm really angry with myself. Why do I let people push me around? Why do I meddle in other people's business? Why? Why? Why?

Something in my brain snaps. It all comes crashing down.

As Trevor starts to walk away, I grab him by the back of his hair. He makes a weird sound that I've never heard before. Using all of my strength I smack his head into the wall. Then I do it again. And again. And again. And again. Trevor starts to cry like a little girl. He screams for someone to help him. But I'm not listening. I just keep hitting his head against the wall. Blood's all over the place. It's all over his head. All over my hands. But I don't care. I just don't care.

"Marty!" I hear someone scream. "Stop that right now!"

But I'm not listening to them. I want Trevor to hurt. So I keep smashing his head against the wall. There's blood everywhere. Finally I let go and he falls to the floor. He's crying like a baby. That makes me happy. He deserved it. As he curls into a little ball I kick him in the back. Then I kick him in the butt. Then I kick him in his private place. Before I can do anything else Barbara has her arms around me. She's dragging me back into the classroom. She's screaming at me to stop.

Kids are standing in the classroom doorways. They're looking at Trevor on the floor. They're looking at me as Barbara drags me back into the Sunday School classroom. Some are covering their mouths with their hands. Others are crying. Nobody is helping Trevor. They just let him lay there on the floor. Blood oozes from a cut on his head. His hair is sticky and gross. I can't believe I actually stood up for myself.

But I'm going to get in trouble for hurting him.

I'm going to get in trouble.

And I don't care.

CHAPTER 16

▼

APOLOGIES

They won't let me leave the classroom.

I guess Trevor's hurt pretty bad. I don't really care, though. He deserved what he got. I should have hurt him worse but that would've gotten me in more trouble than what I'm already in. I know I'm in trouble because I can hear people talking about me on the other side of the door. The preacher and his wife are out there talking. Mom's out there, too. Her voice is the loudest. She sounds like she's pretty upset.

"I can't believe this," I hear Mom say. She's really mad. Her voice gets really high whenever she's mad about something. She must be really angry right now because it's really, really high.

There's more talking but I can't understand what they're saying. I really don't want to know what they're saying, anyway. It's probably all bad and it's probably all about me. What about Trevor? None of this would have happened if he'd just left me alone. I don't understand. I was only defending myself from him. Does that make me a bad person? I don't think so. Steve is a bad person because he hurts other people even when they don't do anything to anyone. Dad is a bad person because he yells at me for no reason sometimes. I'm not a bad person.

The classroom door opens. Donald the preacher comes in.

"Hello, Marty," he says. He looks like he's really sad. I guess I made him that way. "Would you like to talk to me?"

I shrug. I don't say anything.

Donald sits down in the chair next to mine. He puts his hands on my knees. He's trying to make me feel safe. Preachers are supposed to be really good people. They help people when they think they've sinned. They also help pregnant teenagers and drug addicts. That's what they do on TV, anyway. I don't know if Donald has ever helped a pregnant teenager or a drug addict before.

"Do you want to tell me what happened out there?" he asks.

I don't say anything.

"Because we'd really like to know," he says. "We're really concerned for you, Marty. Your mom says you've been having trouble at school."

That makes me mad. Mom doesn't have the right to tell anyone about what happened to me at school. That's my business, not hers. I don't mind if she tells Dad or Grandma or even Steve, but I don't like her telling people that aren't a part of my family. Donald is just the preacher of the church we go to. Just because Mom likes him doesn't mean I like him or want to talk to him. She doesn't understand that. She doesn't understand how shy I can be sometimes.

"You really hurt Trevor," he tells me. "He's still crying about it."

"Then he shouldn't have pushed me and called me names," I say. I try to sound really angry. I don't want to sound like a little kid right now.

"Do you think that's a good reason for hurting him?" he asks.

"Yes," I tell him. "Because he wouldn't listen to me."

"Did you ask him to stop?" he asks.

"Yes," I tell him. "I ask him every week. But it doesn't do any good."

"Have you told your mom about this?" he asks.

"She doesn't listen," I tell him. "She doesn't notice anything important." It's true. If she did then she would know about Steve and everything he's done. I don't think most parents notice anything. They just don't ask the right questions.

Donald doesn't say anything for a minute. "Are you at peace with God?"

I don't understand what he means. "What?"

"Have you accepted God into your life?" he asks.

"I guess," I tell him. I don't want to tell him the truth. I don't want a lecture about God and Jesus right now. If he did start preaching to me I don't know what I would do. I'd probably cover my ears and hum a song. That's what I do when I don't want to hear anything. I do it sometimes when Dad is yelling at me. It makes him mad.

"It's a yes or no answer," he says.

"Yes," I say. "I've accepted God into my life."

"Do you think God would approve of what you did this morning?" he asks.

"No," I say. He starts to say something else but I'm not finished yet. "But I don't think he would be proud of Trevor, either."

"You're very right," he tells me. "He's not happy with how Trevor treated you. But two wrongs do not make a right, Marty."

That's an old saying. I've heard Mom and Dad say that for as long as I can remember. "I know that," I tell him. "But how was I supposed to make him stop? I tried asking. I tried telling. What else was I supposed to do?"

"Tell someone," he says. "Tell an adult."

"That always makes things worse." It's true. If someone at school finds out you told a teacher on them, they'll beat you up and tell everyone about it. I've seen it happen before. It's one of the worst thing you can do at school.

"Did you even try?" he asks.

"No," I say. "Because it never helps."

"But did you even try?" he asks again.

I'm getting tired of his questions. "I told you no."

We don't speak for a while.

"We're not out to get you," Donald tells me. "We're not trying to get you in trouble. We're actually trying to prevent you from getting into trouble in the future. You can't go around beating up people if they say something you don't like."

"He pushed me first," I tell him. "Aren't I allowed to push him back?"

"No," he says. "You're supposed to tell an adult. They can handle the situation much better than you can. Do you understand?"

"No," I say. I'm just being honest. I really don't understand. "Some people say that you have to stick up for yourself. Isn't that true?"

"Sometimes," he says. "But never with violence."

I'm tired of looking at his face. He sweats too much. His glasses keep sliding down his nose because it's so sweaty. His breath is pretty bad, too. I bet he doesn't brush his teeth when he gets up in the morning. That's the only way his breath could smell so bad. For a preacher he doesn't look too sharp. Most preachers on TV are very handsome, very clean, and very dry. Donald isn't handsome, he isn't very clean, and he's not dry. I'm surprised that Donald's allowed to preach at this church. Most of the people who go here aren't very nice to ugly, sweaty people.

"Would you like to apologize to Trevor?" he asks.

"No," I tell him.

He looks like he's losing his patience with me. "Why not?"

"Because he hasn't apologized to me," I say. "Don't you understand that this isn't my fault? This is all Trevor's fault."

"It's both your faults," he tells me. "Both of you were in the wrong."

"I'm not in the wrong," I tell him. "I'm in the right because I stuck up for myself when he was picking on me. Maybe he won't do it anymore."

"And what if he does pick on you again?" he asks.

I look right into his little blue eyes. "Then I'll beat his head into the wall again. I'll do it every time he picks on me until he learns his lesson." I'm not kidding. If Trevor picks on me again I'll beat his head into the wall.

"That's not what I wanted to hear," he says. Then he sighs. "I need to know that you won't do this again in the future."

"I can't tell you that," I tell him. "Because I might end up lying."

Donald's face is beginning to turn red. I think he's getting upset. I always seem to make people upset. "Listen to me very carefully, Marty. Using violence in your youth will lead to a violent future. You have to learn at an early age that you can't solve problems by fighting. You have to sit down and talk them out. It's the only way."

"It's not the only way," I say. "I solved my problem by beating up Trevor."

Donald just shakes his head. "I don't think I can reach you," he says. "You seem to be set in your ways. It makes me sad to see such a young man so angry."

I don't know what to say.

Donald stands up and scoots his chair under the table. "If you want to talk about things realistically, you always know where you can find me. I'm going outside to speak with your mother some more. Wait here until we call for you."

"That's fine," I say.

Right before he leaves the room, he stops in the doorway. I can see Mom out in the hall. "Are you sure you don't want to apologize?"

"Not if I don't get an apology, too," I tell him. "I'm not sorry if he's not sorry."

Donald nods and leaves. He shuts the door behind him.

I hear them talking behind the door again. Their voices are louder this time. When someone's voice is loud that usually means they're excited, angry, or happy. I don't think they're excited and I definitely don't think they're happy. Mom's voice is the loudest, too. I don't even want to see her right now. I can see her angry face in my mind. I can see her angry eyes giving me dirty looks. I'd love to go home and crawl under the covers. I wish I could forget all about church and Trevor and everything.

Then the classroom door opens.

Trevor and his mom come inside. She's really fat, has really ugly hair, and probably sweats more than Donald does. She also breaths through her mouth. Trevor has a large bandage around his head. The bandage is stained with blood. They stand in the doorway, his mom's hands on his shoulders. He won't look at me.

"What do you say?" she says to Trevor.

"Sorry," he snaps. He doesn't really mean it.

His mom slaps him in the back of the head. I bet that hurt. "Say it like you mean it, boy," she says. She sounds worse than my mom.

"Sorry," he says again. This time it actually sounds like he means it.

"Do you have something you'd like to say?" she asks me.

I look at her for a second. She's not my mom. She's not my teacher. She doesn't have any authority over me. "Do it again and I'll beat up you again," I say.

Her mouth drops open. She takes Trevor with her as she leaves the room. The door is slammed shut behind her. I guess I screwed up again but I really don't care. People like Trevor should be killed so they can't bother anyone else. It would make the world so much better. I know I'm going to get in trouble for smarting off to Trevor's mom. I'll never hear the end of it.

I look around the classroom while they talk out in the hallway. There are pictures of Jesus with long hair all over the walls. There's also the Ten Commandments. I know all of them by heart. There are also posters stating the Golden Rule. The Golden Rule is that you should treat others as you would like to be treated. It's really hot down here, too. I guess they don't have air conditioning like we do at home. I'm getting really tired of sitting down here by myself.

Finally Mom comes in the room. She kneels down in front of me and sighs. I can tell by the look on her face that she's not happy with me. "We're leaving," she says. "I hope you're happy. We're going to miss the sermon."

"I don't care," I tell her.

"You don't care?" she asks. "What the hell's gotten into you, Marty?"

I don't answer her.

"Well?" she asks.

"I'm ready to go home now," I tell her. I stand up. "Can we leave?"

"After you tell Trevor you're sorry," she says. "I can't believe you told his mother that you'd beat her son up again. What's wrong with you?"

"What's wrong with you?" I ask.

Mom just looks at me. "Come on," she says. "Let's go apologize."

Mom walks me into the hallway. She's got her hands on my shoulders just like Trevor's mom. Her grip is pretty tight and it's starting to hurt. I don't tell her that, though. I don't want her to know that's she's causing me any problems. I don't want Mom to win arguments anymore. I'm tired of people always winning and me always losing. From now on I'm going to make sure I always win. No matter what.

She moves me in front of Trevor. He's still not looking at me. He's looking at the floor. "I'm sorry," I tell him. I don't even try to sound like I mean it. I feel Mom's hands tighten around my shoulders. She's trying to tell me something without actually saying it.

"Like you mean it, young man," she tells me.

Donald and Trevor's mom are looking at me. They're looking at me like I'm some sort of demented little monster that goes around bashing people's heads into the walls all the time. That's not true. I try to stay out of everyone's way so that stuff like this won't happen. I always seem to find myself surrounded by mean, ugly people. Like right now. Donald is ugly and mean. Trevor's mom is ugly and mean. And even though Mom's not that ugly, she certainly is mean sometimes.

I look at Trevor until he looks up at me. I can't tell if he's scared or not. It does look like his head hurts, though. All those blood stains on the bandage make me feel a little proud. Instead of just getting hit and taking it like a wimp, I stood up for myself and did some damage of my own. It may not have been as evil as what Steve does, but it's good enough for me.

"I hope you go to Hell," I tell Trevor.

Everyone gasps.

I guess that wasn't the right thing to say, either.

"Marty!" Mom says.

"Your son needs serious help," Trevor's mom tells my mom. "I will make sure that everyone knows what type of son you're raising."

"I'm sorry you feel that way," Mom says to Trevor's mom. "It's not like your son is some sort of Boy Scout, either. He's just as rotten."

"My husband will be in touch with yours," Trevor's mom says. "After we have him looked over by our family physician, you can expect the bill in the mail."

"I'm sure we won't have any trouble affording it," Mom tells her.

This makes Trevor's mom really angry. I can tell because her hands start to shake and her face looks really tense. Donald just shakes his head and rubs his forehead. I'll bet this is the first time anything like this has happened in his church. I guess that's why he doesn't know how to handle it. Instead of quoting things from the Bible and telling everyone to be nice, he just shakes his sweaty head and keeps his mouth shut. I'm not very proud that he's my preacher. I'd rather listen to the guys on TV. At least they seem to know how to deal with bad situations.

"You give us a call," Mom says. Then she leads me out of the basement.

We walk all the way through the church with her hands on my shoulders. Every time I start to go in the wrong direction, she digs her nails into my skin. It really hurts. My uncles and aunts and cousins and everyone are seated in the pews. They're waiting for Donald to come out and give the sermon. They watch as Mom leads me out of the church.

We walk to the car in silence.

I don't know what's going to happen to me now.

▼

CHAPTER 17

TWIST

Mom's not paying much attention to the road.

That's because she's mad at me.

Really, really mad.

"I've never been so embarrassed in my entire life!" she screams. Mom doesn't scream very often. But she's really disappointed in me for beating Trevor's head against the wall. I still think he deserved it. Mom doesn't agree with me.

"What was I supposed to do?" I ask. "Let him beat me up?"

"You should have told your teacher," she tells me. "Barbara would have taken care of him. You didn't have to do what you did, Marty."

I disagree but I don't say anything.

Usually after church we stop by Arby's so I can get a roast beef sandwich. She doesn't stop this time. She doesn't even offer to stop. I guess this is my punishment for sticking up for myself. I don't care, though. Trevor deserved what he got and I feel good for doing it. Dad will probably yell at me but I don't care about that, either. He can yell all he wants. I'm tired of being the kid that always gets pushed around. They should be happy that I'm starting to grow up.

Mom stops at a red light. "I just can't believe it, Marty. What's gotten into you?"

"I dunno," I say. "I'm just tired of getting picked on."

"Kids get picked on, Marty!" she yells. "I'm sorry that it happens to you but it's not an excuse to attack someone. Do you understand?"

"No, I don't," I say. "If I tell the teacher then it only gets worse. You just don't understand. I don't know why I'm talking to you."

Mom slaps me across the face. I guess I pushed my luck too far. My cheek stings like crazy. I try not to cry because I don't want to look like a little boy. I'm tired of looking like a little boy. I think of *Morrowind* and other things that make me happy. Even though my eyes are burning the tears don't come. They just disappear. I don't want her to see me cry. That would mean she's won.

"You're just like the rest of them," I tell her. "You hit me, too."

Mom doesn't say anything.

After a few minutes, Mom takes a deep breath. "I'm sorry for slapping you," she says. "But I honestly don't know what to do with you."

"I don't know what to do, either," I tell her. "I'm just trying to stick up for myself. And nobody seems to understand that I'm tired of getting picked on."

"I know you are, sweetie," she says. She's trying to get back on my good side. It's not going to work. "But you have to suffer the consequences for your actions."

"And what about Trevor? What are the consequences for his actions? If I didn't beat his head against the wall, nothing would have happened to him." I'm dead serious. Mom knows it, too. We don't say anything as we pull into the driveway.

"Are you gonna tell Dad?" I ask.

"I have to," she tells me. "We don't keep secrets from each other."

"But this doesn't have anything to do with him," I say. "He doesn't even go to church. Why does he have to know?"

Mom thinks about it for a second. "I'm sorry, Marty. I have to."

"No, you don't," I say. Dad's gonna yell at me. He's gonna be really upset that I hurt Trevor and that he has to pay for the doctor's bill.

I get out of the van and shut the door. Mom follows me into the house. Dad's already in the living room with his hands on his hips. His face is red and he looks like he's ready to yell at someone. Mom closes the door and puts her coat and scarf on the hook. I don't take off my coat. If Dad hits me, it might soften his punch. It's my armor.

"I just got off the phone with Trevor's parents," he says. "Care to explain yourself? Because it sounds like you're in deep shit."

He's talking to me. "He was picking on me. I beat him up."

"You beat him up?" he asks. I don't know why he's asking me if I did it or not. I've already told him I did. Parents are weird sometimes.

"Yeah I did," I tell him.

He slaps me across the face. It's on the same side Mom slapped me. She starts to say something but Dad holds up his hand. "I'll handle this," he tells her. Then he turns back to me. "How did that feel, huh? Did it hurt?"

"No," I say. I won't let him win.

Dad's eyes get really small. His face gets even redder. I think he might kick me through the wall. "I understand that people pick on you, Marty, but you can't just go around beating people up. What if you killed him, huh? What then?"

"I don't care," I say. "He deserved what he got."

He smacks me again. I can taste blood in my mouth. "Don't smart off to me, boy. I'm not playing games with you. This is serious business."

I'm fed up. I start to yell. "I'm serious, too! People are always picking on me and pushing me around! Why don't they get in trouble? Why don't their parents smack them around? You two are assholes! You don't care about me!"

Dad raises his hand again like he's going to hit me. That's when Steve appears at the top of the stairs. "Don't you hit him again," he says.

Dad looks up at Steve. "Stay out of this, Steve."

"I'm not gonna stand here and let you smack him around because he fought back," he says. "Don't you dare hit him again."

"Steve," Mom says. "Go back to your room."

"No," he says. He starts walking down the stairs. "I'm not kidding. Marty's been through enough this week. Just leave him alone."

"I don't recall asking you anything!" Dad shouts at the top of his lungs. I'm sure the neighbors can hear everything we're saying. They know that Dad hit me and they know I don't care anymore. "Just stay the fuck outta this!"

Steve stops at the bottom of the stairs. "I'm not kidding with you, Dad. Leave him alone and go back to your TV. Marty's been through enough."

Dad shoves Steve against the wall. "Go upstairs or get the fuck out." Dad means business. But I can see something in Steve's eyes.

Something horrible.

Steve slaps Dad's hands out of the way. "You touch me again and you're gonna regret it for the rest of your fucking life."

"Oh, really?" Dad says. He shoves Steve again.

Then Steve punches him right in the face.

Blood explodes from Dad's face. Mom screams. Steve punches him in the stomach. Dad vomits air. Steve shoves Dad backwards, making him trip over his own feet. Dad lands on his back. Then Steve kicks him in the ribs. Then he kicks him again. And again. Mom grabs Steve by the shoulder. He grabs her face with his entire hand and pushes her towards the front door. I don't know what to say. I don't know what to think. I've never seen anything like this before in my life.

Steve has completely lost control.

Dad spits blood onto the hardwood floor. His nose won't stop bleeding. Mom's sitting on the floor against the front door. She's crying her eyes out. Steve's right hand is covered in blood. I don't know if it's Dad's blood or his blood. I start to back away from everyone. I'm scared and confused and I don't know what's going to happen next.

"Get out," Dad says. "Get the fuck out."

"No problem," Steve says. He kicks Dad again. For the first time in my entire life, Dad starts to cry. Not like Mom cries, though. It's the silent type of crying. Tears runs through the blood on his face. "If you touch Marty again, it's gonna be much worse."

"Out," Dad says. He sounds like he's in a lot of pain. "Right now."

Steve leans down next to Dad. "I'll be back to deal with you later," he says in a low voice. Dad looks up at him. "I swear to God this isn't over."

Then he grabs his coat from the hook and leaves the house.

I can hear his car pull off down the street.

Mom doesn't stop crying. Dad doesn't stop bleeding. I don't know what to do next. I don't even know what to say. I've never seen anything like that before. Steve doesn't stick up for anyone. Mom says he's the most self-centered person she's ever met. But he proved everyone wrong today. Instead of just standing there and letting Dad smack me around, he stood up for me. It makes me glad that I never said anything to Mom and Dad about the severed heads. It makes me feel good that I have an older brother. I haven't felt that way in a long, long time.

Dad sits down on the bottom step of the staircase. "Go to your room," he tells me. "And don't you dare come out for the rest of the day."

"What about the bathroom?" I ask.

"Don't be stupid," he snaps. "You can go to the bathroom but you're not to come downstairs for any reason. Not even to eat."

I don't care about eating. I'm glad he's hurt.

I just wish I could have been the one to hurt him.

Without saying anything to anyone, I stomp upstairs and go to my room. I slam the bedroom door, too. That way they know I'm angry with them. I sit on the edge of my bed and think about Steve beating up Dad. He just laid him out. It was like watching a boxing match on TV. I've seen people bleed before but I've never seen my parents bleed. It was weird. You never expect to see your parents that way. It's like you don't expect them to bleed like everyone else does. I can't stop thinking about the fight. It plays over and over again in my head.

I wonder if they'll call the cops on Steve? I've seen it happen on TV. Parents that get attacked by their children almost always call the cops. What if they look through Steve's room? What if they find his heads? I don't want to think about that. No telling what might happen if Mom and Dad find out about those severed heads. Would they change the locks? Would they ask the police to sit in front of the house at night just in case he comes back? My life is starting to feel like a horror movie. But I don't know which person is the monster. Is it Steve? Is it Dad?

Is it me?

I turn on my Xbox and play *Morrowind* for a little while. Whenever I see a monster I pretend it's Dad. Then I hack it to death with my broadsword. That's the type of weapon my character uses. Sometimes I use magic, but it's more satisfying to hack them to death with my sword. Since there's a lot of monsters to fight, I have lots of different things to put Dad's head on. I see his head on orcs. I see his head on goblins. I see his head on cliff racers. I see his head everywhere. I'm glad Steve made him hurt. I'm really glad Steve made him cry.

Later on I hear Mom and Dad in Steve's room. I hear hammering. I hear Dad cussing. Since I don't hear any screams I guess they didn't look through his closet. No telling what they're doing in there. They don't spend too much time in Steve's bedroom. Probably about fifteen minutes total. I want to go out into the hallway and see what they're doing. Dad told me to stay in my room so I'm going to stay. I don't want him to slap me across the face again.

Mom and Dad don't come get me when it's time to eat. They eat downstairs by themselves. I can hear their forks and knives scratching across the plates. I can hear them talking, though I can't hear what they're talking about. I wish I could. They're probably talking about me and Steve. They're probably wondering if I'm going to turn out as bad as he did. They don't need to worry about that. I'm not the kind of person to beat up his parents and kill black people. I'm just not.

I open my bedroom door and stick my head out. "I'm hungry!" I yell. "Can I come downstairs and get something to eat?"

"No!" Dad yells. "Stay in your room."

I slam the door.

"And stop slamming doors!" I hear Dad yell.

I lay down on my bed and try not to think about everything that's happening to me. This has been the worst week of my entire life. I can't imagine what else could happen that would make it any worse. Sometimes I wish I could just run away from everything. I wish I could turn eighteen right now and graduate from school. Then I could get a job like Steve and move out on my own. That way Mom and Dad couldn't tell me what to do or smack me around when they think I've been bad. I don't want to be treated like a little kid anymore. I can't take it anymore.

I think about going into Steve's bedroom to get a movie to watch. I don't think I could concentrate on it, though. I've got school to worry about tomorrow. There's always one more thing to worry about. If it's not one thing it's another. That's what Mom always says. I guess she's right. There's always something to worry about. Now that Steve's gone there's nobody here to stick up for me. There's nobody here to give me good advice. And there's nobody to kill the kids that pick on me at school. I'm all alone.

Mom doesn't say goodnight to me tonight. I hear them getting ready for bed, I hear them watching TV, and then I hear them turn off the TV. They must really hate me. I guess they blame me for Dad getting beat up by Steve. If I hadn't beat Trevor's head against the wall at church then none of this would have happened. We'd eat dinner in peace, watch TV in peace, and tell each other goodnight like we always do. They must really hate me.

I listen to my clock radio. I don't even bother to get under the sheets. I just lay on top of my bedspread and look at the posters on my ceiling. They don't help calm me down anymore. They used to make me think of being a filmmaker or writing books for a living. That seems like a long time ago. I don't feel like myself anymore. I'm mean. I'm violent. I'm sick to death of the way people treat me.

Just as my clock radio turns off, I hear a knock at my window. At first I'm horrified. Watching horror movies has made me paranoid of what's outside at night. I get off the bed and slowly walk to the window. There's another knock. It's louder than the last one. I pull open my drapes to find Steve standing outside. He must be really steady because you can easily fall off the roof near my window. It slopes down towards the front yard. You'd get hurt if you fell off it.

I carefully open my window. I don't want Mom and Dad to hear.

"What are you doing?" I ask. I'm pretty happy to see Steve. I didn't know when or if I'd actually see him again.

"I need to get in my room," he tells me. "Mom and Dad nailed the window shut and I forgot my keys. I need to get some stuff."

"Where are you staying?" I ask.

Steve just looks at me. "At a hotel. Can I come in?"

I step out of the way so Steve can crawl through the window. Once he's inside I carefully close it back. "Sorry. I was just worried."

"Are you okay?" he asks.

"I'm okay," I tell him. "What about you?"

"I'll survive," he says. "Don't worry about me, okay?"

I can't help but worry about Steve. He's my big brother.

I follow him into his bedroom.

CHAPTER 18

▼

VIOLENCE

I sit down on the edge of Steve's bed.

He kneels down in front of me. His whole attitude has changed. His eyes keep twitching and he can't seem to keep himself under control. He rubs his hands together nervously like I do when I have to give an oral. The clothes he's wearing are dirty and they smell like they haven't been washed in weeks. Something's going on inside of Steve. Something that I don't think I'm going to like. He just keeps looking at me.

"I need you to stay in my room," he tells me.

"I thought you just needed to pick up some stuff?" I ask.

"I lied," he tells me. "I need you to stay in my room tonight."

"Why?" I ask.

"I just need you to," he says.

"Why?" I ask again. I'm starting to get nervous.

"I need your bed," he tells me. Then he sighs. "Your bed is stronger than mine."

"Not really," I tell him. "I've jumped on them both."

Steve smiles. "Trust me. My bed is really, really old. Yours is in much better condition than mine. That's why I need to use it."

"But why?" He still hasn't answered my question.

There's something in his eyes that I don't like. It's almost like I'm not even talking to Steve. Maybe he's on something. I don't think that Steve does drugs, though. But I really don't know much about Steve anymore. He used to be a nice guy with good thoughts and lots of girlfriends. Now he's a killer that wants to use my bed for some reason. Why does he want to use my bed? Why isn't he telling me why he wants to use it? I just sit and stare at him for a little while. He stands up and looks down at me. I'm afraid that he might hit me like he did Dad.

"Just stay in here. Please." He sounds like he's trying to be nice even though his temper is getting bad. "I need you to stay in here."

"No," I tell him. "I've gotta go to school in the morning. I need to get some sleep."

"You can sleep in my bed," he tells me. "It's comfortable."

"I have a hard time sleeping in strange beds," I lie. I really don't, though. Whenever I spent the night at David's I never had trouble falling asleep. But it's different in Steve's room. David doesn't have a severed head in his closet. He doesn't murder black people. He doesn't beat up his parents.

Steve clenches his fist. "Please. I'm asking you nicely, Marty."

"School's gonna be hard tomorrow," I tell him. "People are gonna talk about me. I just wanna sleep in my bed. It's my bed."

"But I need it!" he snaps. "Don't you understand?"

I don't understand. He's starting to lose control. He's gonna start yelling and screaming and acting up like he did earlier tonight. I'm scared of Steve. He's capable of anything. I can tell by the look on his face that I'm getting on his nerves. He just stands there and stares down at me. It's like he's looking at some-one he doesn't even know. Maybe he doesn't recognize me. Maybe whatever's in his head that's making him crazy has completely taken over. Maybe Steve is dead.

"I don't understand," I tell him. "I just want to go to sleep."

"Sleep in my bed!" he yells. He's being loud. Mom and Dad are going to know he's in the house. No telling what will happen if Dad comes in here. They've already fought once. They might kill each other if they fight again.

"I don't want to sleep in your bed!" I yell back. I'm not putting up with his crap. I'm not putting up with anyone's crap anymore. People aren't going to push me around anymore. That includes Mom and Dad and Steve. I mean it.

Steve grabs me by my shoulders. "Listen to me," he says. "Something's going to happen tonight that's going to change everything. I need you to stay in my room. It's important that you stay out of the way."

"Why?" I ask.

"Because I don't want to hurt you," he tells me.

"Are you going to hurt Mom and Dad?" I ask.

Steve doesn't say anything. He just keeps staring at me.

"Are you going to hurt Mom and Dad?" I ask again.

"Yes," he finally says. He closes his eyes. "They're bad people, Marty. They hate me and they hate you. They act like they'd be happy if they never had us. Dad treats you like shit and Mom treats you like a baby. Aren't you tired of that?"

I don't say anything. Steve shakes me.

"You've got to be tired of that," he says. "It's a horrible way to live. I'm going to free you. I'm going to free the both of us."

"Are you going to kill them?" I ask.

Steve looks at me right in the eyes. "Yes."

I'm starting to sweat. I want to rub the palms of my hands together but Steve's got a firm grip on my shoulders. I can't move my arms. All I can do is look at Steve and wonder why he's acting like this. Mom and Dad don't deserve to die. They might not be the best parents in the world but I do love them. I don't want anything bad to happen to them. I don't want to open Steve's closet and find Mom and Dad's heads in the bowling ball bag. I don't want that to happen.

I jerk away from Steve. "I don't want you to kill them, Steve."

"They hurt you," he tells me. "They hurt me. It's time for them to learn that they can't do this to people. I won't stand for it anymore."

I try to stand up but Steve pushes me back down. "Stop it, Steve."

"Please," he says. He's begging. You can hear it in his voice. "Please don't make this any harder. I don't want anything to happen to you."

"I'll call the police," I tell him.

"Don't even joke like that," he snaps. He shoves me. "I'll hurt you, Marty. Please don't make me do that. Please."

"I swear I will," I say. "They'll lock you away forever."

"You wouldn't do that to me, would you? I'm your big brother." I know what he's trying to do and it's not going to work.

"If you cared you wouldn't do this to me," I tell him. "You're no different than the people who pick on me. And that includes Dad, too."

Steve shoves me back onto the bed and puts his knee on my chest. I think I'm going to die because I can't get a good, deep breath. I try to push him off me but he's too strong and too heavy. I think I made him mad when I compared him to Dad. Steve hates Dad so I can see why that would make him angry. I don't care. It's the truth. He's going to ruin my life. What would happen to me if Mom and Dad died? What would I do? Where would I live? I don't want to think about it.

"Don't fuck with me," he says. His voice is low and harsh. He means business now. "I need to do this. I need this. I need it."

"Why?" I ask.

"Because they are everything I hate," he says. "Because Mom and Dad are terrible parents. They're worse than those fucking niggers, Marty. They're mean to us and they didn't do a very good job of raising us."

"I think they did fine," I tell him. I try to sound like I'm mad, too. But my voice keeps cracking because his knee is in my chest. "Just because they don't act like other parents doesn't mean they didn't do a good job."

Steve presses harder on my chest. "They did a good job? Look at me! I'm fucked up, Marty, and they never raised a hand to help. They never noticed. And you! Look at you! You don't even get upset when you find someone's severed head in your brother's closet. All of those horror movies have warped you, Marty. They've ruined you."

"No they haven't," I shout. "Get off me!"

"Be quiet!" he snaps. "Don't you dare wake up Mom and Dad."

"Help!" I scream. "Help me!"

He presses down even harder on my chest. I can barely breath. "I told you to keep quiet. Say one more thing and I'll fucking gut you."

I try to speak but it's too hard. His knee is cutting off my air.

The bedroom door opens.

Dad stands in the doorway.

"What the fuck is going on in here?" he yells.

Steve gets off me and turns to Dad. "Stay outta this." He points right at Dad.

"Stay outta something that's happening in my own house? You've got some nerve," Dad says as he moves in close. Steve doesn't move at all. "How the hell did you get back in here, anyway? We nailed your fucking windows shut!"

"Marty let me in," he says.

Dad looks at me. "Is that true?"

I don't say anything.

"I asked you a goddamn question!" Dad shouts.

"Hey!" Steve shouts back. He's still pointing his finger at Dad's face. "Don't talk to him that way. He was only helping out his older brother."

"He should know better than to help you," Dad says. "And keep your goddamn finger outta my face, you got that?"

Steve lowers his finger, nods, and then punches Dad right in the face. Again. Dad yelps, grabs his nose, and stumbles out of the room. He leans back against the railing in the hallway. I'm afraid he might fall over and hurt himself. I stand up just as Steve goes into the hall. My chest is killing me but it feels good to take a deep breath again. Just as I join them in the hallway Mom comes out of their bedroom.

"What's going on?" she asks in a sleepy voice.

"Call the police!" Dad says. His voice is muffled because his hands are over his face. Blood drips from his chin.

"Shut-up!" Steve yells. He shoves Dad back against the railing. He's gonna fall all the way down to the first floor. I just know it.

"Stop it!" Mom screams. "You're gonna kill him!"

Steve turns his anger towards Mom. She backs up towards her bedroom. "You'd better stay away or you'll get it worse than him."

Steve rubs his privates. I can see his penis bulging through his jeans.

I can't believe what's happening.

"You've lost your mind!" I scream. "Just stop it!"

Steve's not listening to me anymore. He's not listening to anyone. Something else has control of his body and his voice. This isn't the Steve we know at all. This is a stranger in our house wearing Steve's skin. Everything I used to love about my big brother is gone. I no longer look up to him. I don't want to be his brother anymore.

I know exactly what I have to do.

Even though my chest is killing me I start running at Steve. He doesn't even see me heading towards him. Before he knows what's happening I hit him in the stomach with my right shoulder. Steve hits the railing. It bends, creaks, and snaps. Both he and Dad go flying through the air.

I hear them hit the floor below.

"No!" Mom screams. She runs down the stairs.

"Don't go down there!" I shout. "Mom!"

Mom's not listening, though. She's too worried about Dad and Steve.

She runs downstairs to help them. It's not a good idea. If Steve is still able to get up then she's in danger of getting hurt. I lean over the broken railing and look down at them. Dad's out cold. Steve's starting to get up. I yell at Mom but she's not listening to me. She just keeps heading towards them. She's going to get hurt. I try to tell her this but she just won't listen to me. Why won't she listen to me? Doesn't she understand that I'm trying to help her? Doesn't she understand?

When Mom gets to the bottom of the stairs, Steve grabs her by the hair and slings her into the wall. I hear the thump and then I hear her cry out. Dad's still not moving. Steve takes Mom's head and bangs it against the wall. Then he does it again. And again. I don't know if she's still alive. I feel helpless. I feel like this is all my fault.

I guess it's too late for that now.

There's only one thing I can do.

I have to stop Steve.

I run downstairs and grab Steve around the waist and try to pull him off Mom. There's blood on the wall where her head has hit it. Steve gets between her legs and begins rubbing himself against her body like he's trying to have sex with her. And I can't make him stop. I can't pull him off her. I just can't make him stop. He's too strong for me. I take a few steps back and try to kick him in the privates. The only thing that does is make him mad. He grabs me by the face and shoves me backwards. I trip over Dad and hit my head against the wall. It hurts like crazy. Everything gets blurry.

That's the last thing I remember.

Until I wake up.

CHAPTER 19

▼

CONCLUSIONS

It's dark in here.

I'm tied to Steve's bed.

From what I can tell Dad's tied to my bed. At least I think he is. I can hear him screaming for Mom from my bedroom. But Mom's making noise, too. I can hear her groaning and moaning from her bedroom. Since she's not running around or trying to leave I'm guessing that she's tied up, too. I think Steve is having sex with her. It sounds like it does in the movies. But I don't think Mom is enjoying it. She's crying out and groaning like something is hurting her really bad. I wish I could get up and make Steve stop hurting her. I can't stand the sound she's making.

"Lisa!" Dad yells. "Please answer me!"

"Stanley!" Mom yells. She sounds horrible. "Help me!"

"I will!" I hear Dad scream. He's crying, too. "I'm going to help you!"

He has to know he can't help her. If he's tied up like I'm tied up he's not going anywhere. Steve's used some sort of leather strap to hold us down. When I try to move my arms it hurts. When I try to move my legs it hurts. When I try to move my neck it hurts. I can't even talk. There's a ball in my mouth that's held in place by a leather strap that wraps around my head. I keep slobbering around the ball. I try to spit it out but I can't. It tastes like rubber. I want to spit it out so bad that my tongue starts to hurt.

"Stanley!" Mom screams.

"Love it! Love it! Love it!" I hear Steve tell her. He's groaning and moaning, too. But it sounds like he's enjoying himself. He keeps laughing that crazy laugh. I can hear the bed squeaking. It echoes through the house.

I wish I couldn't hear anything.

The groaning and moaning and screaming and squeaking keeps going and going. Going and going. It's all I can hear. Every so often Dad will yell out something. He's just trying to help Mom feel better. Maybe if she thinks that someone is coming to save her then she'll be okay. But I don't think we're ever going to be okay again. Steve has gone too far this time. I don't think anything will be the same.

Then, all of a sudden, the squeaking stops.

I hear footsteps. They're coming towards the bedroom. The door opens and Steve comes in. He's completely naked. His penis is sticking straight out like a faucet. He walks over to the closet and opens the doors. He's looking for something. It's just like that night I was hiding under his bed. What's he looking for? All of the lights are out so I can't see a thing. All I can see is the outline of Steve's naked body. He starts tossing things out of his closet. He throws clothes on top of me. He throws old magazines on top of me. He even throws a few old school books on top of me.

I try to talk but I can't with the ball in my mouth.

"Don't try to talk," Steve says. He doesn't even turn around. "You'll gag."

I try to say something. I gag just like Steve said I would.

"Be quiet!" he snaps. Then he takes something out of the closet. I can't tell what it is because it's so dark in here. Without saying anything else, he walks out of the room. He doesn't close the door behind him. I can hear his feet go pat-pat-pat across the hardwood floor. He's heading back to Mom and Dad's bedroom.

Then Mom screams.

"Lisa?" Dad yells. "Lisa! Are you all right?"

"Help me, Stanley!" she screams. "Please! He's going to kill me!"

"Steve!" Dad cries out. "Please! We can talk about this, son! You don't have to do this!" But I don't think Steve's listening right now.

Mom starts to say something else but it ends in a horrible scream. It's a scream I've heard a hundred times in a hundred different horror movies. And even though I've heard it before on TV it's worse in real life. And she doesn't stop screaming. She just screams and screams. Each one is worse than the one before it. I want to cover my ears but I can't. I try to move my arms but I can't. Dad keeps yelling and he won't stop. Everything is going crazy. My head won't stop buzzing.

"I love you!" Dad yells. "Sweetie, I love you!"

Mom doesn't answer him. She just keeps screaming.

"I love you!" Dad screams at the top of his lungs. "Nothing will change that! Nothing!" He starts crying really hard. Like when I fall off my bike or something and skin my knee. That's how hard he's crying.

I want to tell Mom I love her, too. I want to tell her I'm sorry for being such a bad son. I want to tell her that it's my fault everything is falling apart. I want to tell her that I wish I could have been better at being a kid. But I can't. That ball is keeping me from saying anything. All I can do is drool on myself. I start to cry.

Then everything goes quiet.

"Lisa?" Dad calls out. "Lisa?!"

"She's dead, Daddy," Steve says. He's laughing when he says it. I think he's still in the same bedroom as Mom. "You should see her, Daddy. She's all dressed up for you. You wanna see? You wanna see?"

"Lisa!" Dad calls out again. "Talk to me, honey!"

I hear Steve's footsteps across the hardwood floor. He's heading to my bedroom. After a few seconds of nothing, I hear Dad scream really loud. He just keeps screaming and screaming. It's the kind of scream when you see something that scares you to death. I don't want to see what Dad sees.

"See?" Steve laughs. "She wants to give you a kiss."

"No!" Dad yells "You fucking bastard! No!"

Then his screaming changes. It goes from a scream of fright to a scream of pain. And the screaming doesn't stop. I try to move but it hurts too much. I want to get up and run away from his place. Steve has lost his mind and he's killing my mom and dad. By the end of the night I won't have anyone left.

I have no friends.

I don't have a big brother.

I don't have parents.

Nobody.

I keep struggling but I know it's no good. The leather straps he's used to hold me down are doing their job. Dad doesn't stop screaming. Even though his screams aren't as nasty as Mom's I know what kind of scream it is. Steve is torturing him. Steve is doing really horrible things to him. I wish I couldn't hear anything. Everything feels unreal. I'm dizzy. If I could pass out right now I would.

Suddenly, everything goes quiet.

Then I hear Steve's footsteps across the hardwood floor.

I hear rustling. I hear movement. What's he doing? I can't tell. There's more movement. The squeaky-squeak of bedsprings. More movement. I strain to hear every little detail. Is he coming in here next? Am I the next victim on his list? I don't want to die. I'd rather go to church seven days a week than die. I'd rather show my penis to anyone who wants to look than die.

Steve walks into the bedroom and turns on the overhead light.

At first I can't see anything because my eyes are all squinty.

Then, after a few seconds, I see everything.

Steve is soaked with blood. Gore. Stuff I've only seen in movies. There are big pieces of skin hanging from his mouth. His hair has little white chunks in it. His penis is still sticking straight out. It's covered in blood. He looks like something out of a nightmare. I want to scream but I can't. I want to run but I can't. The leather straps are starting to make my skin hurt. Is he going to kill me next?

"You can't understand right now," he says. He's talking really weird. "In the morning, you'll understand."

I start to cry.

I can't believe this is happening.

My parents are dead.

They're dead. And he killed them.

"I'm sorry," he tells me. He kneels down next to me. There's pieces of skin between his teeth. "But you'll thank me for this when you're older. You'll see. Everything's going to be okay."

It's not going to be okay. I can't tell him that, though.

He brushes my cheek with the back of his hand. "I'm sorry about all of this," he says. "I really am. You know I wouldn't do anything to hurt you, right? I'm your big brother! I let you borrow my movies!"

There's something wrong with him. He doesn't sound right. His voice keeps going up and down. He rubs his forehead a lot and he keeps looking around the room like he's waiting for something to jump out and get him. And he's not making any sense. I'd never thank him for this. I never wanted him to kill Mom and Dad. I never wanted him to tie me to his bed. I never wanted anything but for us to be a family again. I would tell him everything but I can't. I'll gag if I try to talk.

"You deserve to know what happened," he tells me. He sounds very serious. "I'll show you in the morning, okay? I'll show you everything."

He's not making any sense. I cry even harder.

"Please stop crying," he whines.

I can't stop crying.

"Stop crying," he tells me. He means business.

But I can't stop crying.

"Stop crying!" he shouts. He puts his hands over his ears and scoots away from the bed. "I didn't make you cry! I didn't make you sad!"

He did, though. This is his fault. All his fault.

"Stop it!" he says over and over again. He's crying, too. He starts beating on his head with his fists until the skin around his scalp is red. Snot hangs from his nose and tears run through the blood on his face.

Suddenly Steve jumps to his feet. He screams at the top of his lungs as he pulls out a large chunk of hair from his head. Then he runs out of the room and stomps down the stairs. I hear him open the front door and slam it shut. Wearing nothing but Mom and Dad's blood, he runs off down the street. I know this because I can hear him screaming all the way down. Someone's going to call the cops for sure.

Then everything starts to blur.

I'm getting dizzy.

I doesn't seem real. It can't be real. Maybe it's just a movie. A horror movie. And horror movies never end good.

I can't stop crying. My brain's not working right. All I can think about is Mom and Dad and all the times we spent together. All the vacations we went on. All of the fun times we had together. I want to be a family again. I want us to sit around the TV and watch the sitcoms Dad wants to watch and eat popcorn and laugh when the audience laughs. I just want everything to be normal again.

I want to be normal again.

I'm suddenly tired. I can barely keep my eyes open. I want to stay awake so I can try to get up but I just don't have the energy. It's like someone turned off the power to my brain or something. I stop crying and try to sniff up all the snot in my nose. Then I drift off to sleep. I just drift away.

*   *   *   *

I'm all alone.

The lights are out.

Piled on the bed all around me are the severed limbs of Mom and Dad. The sheets are soaked with blood. I try to move but I can't. Those leather straps are still holding me in place. I can barely turn my head. That's probably a good thing. Sitting on both sides of my pillow are the severed heads of my parents. They're both turned so that they're looking at me. Their eyes have been cut out.

Their mouths are open in a scream. I guess they're supposed to be watching over me.

Sunlight is starting to creep through the drapes.

Monday is here.

School will be starting soon.

Will anyone notice I'm gone? Will anyone notice that Dad's not at work? Will anyone notice that Mom's not at work? When will they decide to search the house? When will I be freed? Until then I'm here with the severed heads of my parents. They're watching over me. It makes me feel comfortable. Special. I try to talk to them through the gag in my mouth but I can't. All I do is drool on myself.

I don't hear anything else in the house. I guess Steve is gone for good. I wonder if the police will ever catch him. I wonder if he'll keep killing black people. All I can do is wonder. All I can do is think about what's going to happen.

I have no idea what's going to happen.

I try to move my legs but it hurts.

I try to move my arms but it hurts.

I try to move my head but it hurts.

I look over at Mom. She's screaming at me with empty eyes. I look over at Dad. He's yelling at me with empty eyes. Their arms and legs and skin and bones and blood are all over the bed. All over me. My mind wants to scream and kick and freak out but I keep myself under control. If I lose it now I might not come back for a long, long time. Stuff like this can really warp a person. That's what Dad says.

Dad.

Mom.

Steve.

I start crying again.

The sunlight's coming through the window.

And I can't stop crying.

0-595-33064-9

Made in the USA
Columbia, SC
26 April 2024

34926592R00083